THE TROUBLE WITH TIME TRAVEL

SEVEN RULES OF TIME TRAVEL
—— BOOK 2 ——

ROY HUFF

This book is fiction. Historical events have been modified.
Any resemblance to real names, events,
persons, or organizations is purely coincidental.

Cover and formatting by Damonza.com

Copyright © 2021 by Roy Huff
All Rights Reserved.

To download your FREE copy of *Salvation Ship*, visit
Roy Huff at https://royhuff.net/salvationship/

This book is dedicated to those who lost their
lives and livelihoods in 2020 and 2021.

CONTENTS

Chapter 1 1
Chapter 2 5
Chapter 3 10
Chapter 4 14
Chapter 5 26
Chapter 6 33
Chapter 7 38
Chapter 8 46
Chapter 9 56
Chapter 10 65
Chapter 11 83
Chapter 12 93
Chapter 13 103
Chapter 14 110
Chapter 15 121
Chapter 16 130
Chapter 17 140
Chapter 18 148
Chapter 19 154
Chapter 20 165
Chapter 21 173
Chapter 22 183
Chapter 23 189
Chapter 24 200
Chapter 25 206
Chapter 26 213
Chapter 27 221
Chapter 28 226
Chapter 29 231

Don't forget to visit the link below for your FREE copy of *Salvation Ship*:

https://royhuff.net/salvationship/

CHAPTER 1

August 7, 2021, Day 1, Timeline 2
7:32 a.m.

QUINN STARED AHEAD until Cameron's tight grip shook him from his stupor. The last thing he remembered was gazing up at the sky toward the array in 2025 after his phone conversation with Jeremy, but Quinn knew the exact time he'd arrived. It was seared into his brain for all of eternity. The full brunt of the supernova was seconds away.

Quinn squinted, uncertain how he'd returned to the main event. Four years flew by since Quinn successfully saved mankind, and in those four years, he'd never been able to pull another *Groundhog Day* or wake up somewhere in his past. So why now?

"Cameron," Quinn said, pausing. She kissed him before he could finish, which he assumed was for the three little words he knew she thought he was thinking. What he really wanted to say was, "Something's wrong." The kiss gave him pause, convincing him to let the array do its thing before giving her the disturbing news.

Quinn's mansion rested on an elevated platform near

Jayne's Hill, Long Island. Lush, wooded pastures surrounded his home. Despite his lavish digs, the estate exuded a lived-in, homey feel, a snug little abode that wasn't constrained by a lack of space. He'd learned the trick from Southern brick architecture. The secret was lots of rooms, so many you could get lost in them. If constructed properly, each room gave off the vibe of its own little cottage.

The master bedroom graced the top floor. Custom windows and sliding doors allowed for either total privacy or panoramic views. From what Quinn remembered, he set the timer the night before to open for maximum viewing just before the event's apex.

A tide of light streamed in. The supernova's brightness exceeded the morning sun, but it was more gradual than Quinn expected, then or now. It was the second time he'd seen it, and both times he marveled at how the brightness rolled in like a calming white wave of ocean water.

Somewhere in space, the array unfolded at that moment, forming a vast network of superthin material designed to use the supernova's leading edge as a factory. As the events progressed, the reaction would catalyze the array's final configuration into material with spatial properties needed for the magnetic stasis field. Microseconds after completion, portions of the newly minted material would condense into segmented storage nodes functioning both as magnets and antimatter storage devices. Quinn knew from the first time, it would work.

Cameron's face beamed in the brightness. "We're not crispy toast right now, so I think it's working."

Quinn forced a smile. Memories flooded his thoughts.

He'd finally gotten some distance from the event and settled into his life as a new space race billionaire. And despite its glamour, he'd managed a humble existence, mansions and spaceship prototypes notwithstanding. "I think you're right," he replied.

Even though it was only four years since the event, it was a couple decades more since his last do-over, and he'd gotten rusty on remembering the subtleties of time jumping. Cameron saw the benefits, but the trouble with time travel was that it was tough to be certain of anything on a second trip.

Quinn attributed the uncertainty to both faulty memory and the butterfly effect. But the closer to an event, the more likely Quinn's memory was the culprit. The brain likes to fill in gaps, which makes memories unreliable. One false recollection is all it takes to end the world. Quinn thought the quote often attributed to Mark Twain summarized it best when it said, "It ain't so much the things that people don't know that make trouble in this world, as it is the things that people know that ain't so."

It was that idea that Quinn managed to impart to the masses after his successful endeavor. The decade prior had been so toxic. When the powers that be drew lines in the sand, people accepted their marching orders and became blind to the truth, unable to believe anything other than what they saw or read from their own tribe. Even successes were deemed failures if they weren't achieved by the right person. They viewed only one side of an equation, one highlighted variable, not comprehending how one action impacted ten others or how attempting to save one life often killed countless more.

Once the array succeeded, he did more than save the

planet. He added perspective. Quinn's actions removed the blinders covering the hidden variables and reignited the waning human spirit. He could only pray his latest time jump hadn't undone all that progress.

CHAPTER 2

August 20, 2025, day 1, timeline 1
8:00 p.m.

NEAR HIS ESTATE, Quinn reclined comfortably next to Cameron on the large picnic blanket underneath the night sky. Cameron wove her fingers into his as they lost themselves in the ocean of twinkling stars near the array, which was visible from most positions on the planet on a clear night.

"We should go up there again and see Jeremy. How long has it been?" she asked.

"Too long," Quinn said, pausing and looking up. "Maybe," he added, "we should call him."

Cameron's eyes widened. Quinn smiled, thinking he'd gotten himself in trouble, walking all over their romantic interlude. "I'm sorry," he said, leaning over as he planted a long, deep kiss on her plump, red lips. He debated on whether to finish the sentence, but she didn't give him the chance to decide.

"No. You're right. I think you should. We haven't seen him or Sam in so long. Find out when he's free, and we should go up there."

Quinn tapped his left temple, activating his phone lens. A three-dimensional holo image of a ringing telephone appeared for both of them to view. After a few moments, Jeremy's face appeared.

"Quinn . . . Cameron! It's great to see you. What's up?"

Quinn went into a long, boring diatribe about his recent starship project before Cameron broke up the monotonous conversation.

"We've been meaning to get up there to see you guys. How's Sam?" Cameron asked, who'd always been protective of her non-binary cousin.

"They're doing fine. It's been a madhouse up here. But funny you should ask. I think we're free tomorrow. First time since I can remember."

Quinn wanted to talk more but figured they would have more time the next day. Over the next few minutes, Quinn wrapped up the conversation and made the arrangements. After hanging up, he tried to resume his lazy discussion of the stars with Cameron, but the short chat with his old friend kept his mind distracted, scattered amongst the numerous timelines he'd lived.

After the call, Jeremy went back to work on the array manipulating the computer holo. His hands moved quickly in unison with the projected images. He wasn't as quick as Sam or Gary, who'd had decades more programming experience, but he was fast enough. Several consecutive indicators displayed the level of energy stored in the array nodes and how much energy they'd used since the supernova loaded its first full charge.

When Quinn looped time, his first big idea was to use the supernova's leading edge to initiate an antimatter reaction, transforming the array into an inverse Dyson sphere. What was once a planet-killing blast of energy became just enough to create a self-sustaining antimatter farm. And once in place, connected nodes could spawn off smaller versions whenever needed. There would initially be enough stored antimatter from the event to last a lifetime based on current use, but if the past was any indication, it would only be a matter of time before that was no longer the case.

Quinn's array company distributed fourteen hundred minifarms since the supernova and stationed most on Earth for research, orbital travel, and more recently, residential use. Several others remained in high orbit for industrial production and various starship manufacturing plants, most nearing completion. Quinn's ship was scheduled to be the first. It was the reason he'd stepped down as CEO and handed off the reins to Jeremy when he did.

For the last year, Jeremy managed the antimatter farm allotment. Sam handled the brunt of the energy flow and high-level tech work, and both used large support teams stationed in various sectors of the array.

Sam and Jeremy worked from the large control center, which had a polished, futuristic design that Quinn had insisted on. He even stole the idea for a massive viewscreen resembling that on the bridge of *Star Trek: The Next Generation's USS Enterprise NCC-1701-D*.

"I need a break," Jeremy said. On his way out, static crackled through the sound system. "What was that?" he said, staring a few seconds too long at the indicators with a blank expression that contrasted with his handsome face.

Sam frowned. "Your guess is as good as mine," they said, pulling up a full status report on the computer holo. "Look at this. Something strange is happening to the energy conduits.

They're pulsating like they're about to overload. But I don't see any surges, and the nodes themselves are all under full capacity." Sam shifted to the right, activating several backup indicators which glowed purple and made their black lipstick and sleek, checkered outfit luminesce.

"Pull up the ambient energy regulators," Jeremy replied. The holo imagery erupted like a New Year's fireworks display. The output readings fluctuated wildly between bone dry and a catastrophic explosion in space.

"What in the world?" Sam said. "This can't be right. I don't believe this. There must be a malfunction somewhere. These numbers are impossible."

"Shut it off. Shut everything off. Let's do a cold boot of the system," Jeremy said.

Even in reboot, skeletal backup systems monitored a few critical readings and could activate or seal off nodes as needed. But in the four years they'd been up there, it never came to that.

The array maintained several backups and manual overrides. And then there was the final option to seal everything off. The distributed minifarms would continue running normally, but the main network would grind to a halt until ambient solar power reinitialized the primary stasis field. The only problem was that the nodes would lose significant energy during reinitialization. Still, it was better than a total loss, but they weren't there yet, just a basic restart to clear the old-school cache.

"Rebooting now," Sam said.

Much like the smell added to natural gas for safety, the array included artificial sound in reboot. The trigger initiated a medium-high-pitched wail that decreased in intensity and lowered in pitch as systems shut down. Within a few moments, they'd gain another crew member in the control center who'd help with overrides and required emergency tech support.

On cue, Gary rolled in from the hallway on power-assisted roller skates blaring Van Halen's "Dance the Night Away" so loud it was audible from his custom earbuds over the array's subsiding wail. He'd upgraded to a slick EverQuest II T-shirt contrasted with work-inappropriate cutoff jean shorts which accentuated his bulging muscled physique. And by this point, he'd swapped hair lengths with Sam, whose hair was now short and bowl shaped, while his was past his shoulders.

"Ah. The benefits of artificial gravity," Gary said. "What's with all the drama?"

"Take a look for yourself," Sam said as Gary rolled up to a station interface. Gary was a beast with tech who could manipulate nearly any screen like a wizard. Sam was on the same level but in different areas.

"Feels just like the old days. Just wish I had a joystick," he said. Sweat trickled down the back of his neck, not from stress or roller-skating down the corridors, but from the intense workout Jeremy knew he'd just completed.

The crackling sound returned. Gary wrinkled his forehead. "So you hear it too," Sam said.

"I do, and it sounds suspiciously analog."

Jeremy was almost finished reaching out to all nine agency heads who frequented the array. "I get the creepy feeling that a poltergeist is about to pop out of the screen," he added.

The main holos flashed in a repeating sequence. Gleaming white alternated with pitch black, and in the short space in between, the crackle returned.

CHAPTER 3

Date and location unknown. Timeline unknown. 9:00 a.m.

QUINN OPENED HIS eyes. A woman lay beside him, hidden under the covers except for one dainty arm draped over the bedside. The lady squirmed. He observed her unfamiliar form. The covers hid her face, but he *could* tell she wasn't his wife. She rolled some more, revealing more of her appearance and stark beauty. His heart thumped.

Quinn slipped off the mattress and meandered around the room, hunting for the slightest clue of where he was and how he got there, before the mysterious woman awoke.

Where . . . or when is here?

Quinn cracked open the curtain. Seductive palm trees, a white-sand beach, and a shallow, crystal clear ocean fronted the low-rise hotel. It would be easy to get lost in the music of the soft, warm sea, but the sinking feeling in the pit of his stomach grew stronger.

This was not his life.

Suffocation replaced what could've been bliss, and he knew from past experience whatever got him to that place could have catastrophic consequences for everyone else. A wave of heat washed over him. His skin warmed, and his mind tried to quell the fear throttling his insides.

Quinn rotated his neck, continuing to inspect the room for anything out of place. After a few fruitless scans, he waddled toward the bathroom, grateful for quiet floor tiling.

Once in the bathroom, he filled his lungs, gripping the sides of the expansive sink, then exhaled. The colorful sample soaps and toothbrush told him the name of the hotel but little else.

"Hungry Like the Wolf" by Duran Duran blared from a passing car radio somewhere outside. His mental control slipped, forcing his heart to skip a beat. He shot up, banging his head on the corner of the open mirror cabinet above him. He grimaced, gripping the sink tighter.

Rustling echoed in from the bedroom. "You there, hun?" a barely audible and disturbingly familiar voice said from the direction of the bed.

"Be there in a sec," he replied, sounding as if he just played a recording of himself instead of speaking the actual words. He inhaled a couple more breaths, uncertain when the situation would come crashing down. He closed the mirror and stole a glance. The reflection was wrong, familiar, but off. Still, the pressing issue at hand demanded his attention. What was he going to tell her, whoever *she* was?

Quinn traipsed toward his side of the bed, silent.

"Should we order room service?" she asked.

He stood for a moment noticing more of himself. His hands and skin looked and felt different, ten years younger maybe. At first, he was certain he'd woken up in the past, but this was no past he remembered. Had he somehow landed in an alternate past, switched lanes in the multiverse with some other version of himself? It didn't fit how he thought time travel worked, with one's holographic mind tethered to only previously lived timelines. But it wasn't inconceivable that he was wrong or missed some critical piece of the puzzle despite the numerous lives he'd already lived.

Her pleasant smile faded the longer he held his reply. "You okay? What's wrong?"

Nothing. Everything.

"Yeah. I'm fine. Room service sounds good."

"You sure you're okay?"

"Maybe just something I ate last night," he replied, having no idea what he had eaten and hoping it didn't set off any red flags. She stared at him. He wondered if she could sense his dishonesty. The irony was, he didn't like to lie, but he'd gotten used to it. His whole life was a lie.

"You good to eat breakfast?" she asked, walking toward him in a plush, white hotel robe. Her appearance was so familiar, but her flawless skin and half-fallen retro hairdo distracted his train of thought. She stepped closer, pressing herself next to him and wrapping her warm, inviting arms around his waist, squeezing.

He stepped back, trying both not to grimace or give in. "Sorry. I think I should be okay to eat. Just a headache, that's all," he said, backing away some more.

She stepped forward. "Maybe what you need is a mimosa," she said, grabbing his right hand.

He'd never cheated on his wife, and he didn't want to start now. His eyes darted away then spotted the hotel menu's leather binding. "Let's see. Bacon and eggs. Crab cakes benedict. What do you think?" he asked, worried it sounded too forced.

"And a couple mimosas," she added, inching closer.

"Can you order? I need to sit down," Quinn said, letting her take over. The excitement in her eyes diminished, and his heart sank. Even though he didn't know who she was or the exact circumstances, he felt bad. He knew it probably wasn't fair to her.

He crumpled onto the comfortable, warm bed and closed his eyes. He found that sometimes, to speed up, one has to first slow down. He only wanted a few seconds, a couple of slow breaths to calm his racing mind. He opened his eyes, hoping to find clarity, but the memory gap remained. Perhaps after he learned his location in fourth-dimensional space, he might be closer to discovering the answer.

The doorbell rang. "Room service," a voice echoed from the other side. She opened the door, allowing the hotel worker to cart in breakfast. The male worker wore a classic getup with striped, dark pants, a matching top, and another retro hairdo. Quinn wasn't sure exactly from which decade, but he had a good idea of the range from all the TV and movies he'd watched.

The hotel charged the food to the room, but he still needed to leave a tip. He fumbled through the top drawer by the bed until he found his wallet and opened up the front flap which housed his driver's license. As soon as he saw the name, he realized why everything was both familiar and off.

"Oh . . . my . . . God!"

CHAPTER 4

The Array. August 20, 2025, day 1, timeline 1
8:17 p.m.

A FLEETING IMAGE appeared on the main screen followed by garbled words. Shortly after, the same image flashed on the holos.

Sam waved their hands, manipulating a 3D holo's interface layers. "What the hell is that?"

"It looked like a person, maybe a message," Jeremy replied.

"That's impossible. This thing is hackproof."

The image reappeared and flickered. Sam dropped their hands and slid back a few steps. The holo transfixed their attention followed by an uncomfortable silence once the reboot's subsiding wail concluded.

"Nothing's hackproof," Gary added, twirling on one wheel as his fingers worked their magic on a separate screen.

"Like I said, poltergeist," Jeremy added.

The image flashed again. This time, a couple audible words slipped through. The holos blinked. Bars appeared, diagonal and moving as if from an old television screen being adjusted for a crisper image.

"I . . . I . . . You . . . You . . ." the image said, cutting in and out. The word "Jeremy" slipped through the crackle.

"Did you hear that? It just called my name. Someone's trying to communicate with us. This shouldn't be possible."

"You heard the words yourself," Gary replied.

For a moment, Jeremy thought someone was pranking him. He wasn't sure who was more of a jokester, Gary or himself. If he had asked that question a decade earlier, it would be himself for sure. But recently, they switched roles. Managing the array since Quinn stepped down forced Jeremy to step up. It wasn't that he resented taking the job, but it was starting to wear him down. Sam wasn't above suspicion either. Sam could pull off jokes deadpan.

"But he's right. This shouldn't be possible. I'm going to run a deep systems check. Whatever's creating this interference could be what's making the indicators go haywire. Let's see what happens after reboot," Sam said.

"Quinn," the message said, interrupting them. Just then, all the indicators stopped and lights vanished. Clicks echoed through the halls, then the lights restarted, beginning from the most distant sections of the adjacent halls until all the lights in the control room lit up at once.

The holos restarted. The static and image faded. "Let's hope that did the trick," Jeremy said.

Gary and Sam remained quiet. They all took in the returning sounds of system clicks as they dove through layers of code.

"You know, this is beautiful. We don't say it enough. Just look at it," Gary added.

Jeremy definitely noticed. It was the tradeoff for working in near isolation. Windows everywhere drank in the pale blue Earth and surrounding stars. It was a dream to move into space, but he wasn't prepared for the psychological adjustment. It reminded him of taking too long of a nap during the day like he was in a perpetual daze, out of sync but not able to place why. Even as the array grew more crowded, the feeling never left.

"So far, so good. Activity on the backup drives is muted, like it should be. Heating systems and magnetic coils are in the green. Energy transfer grids are all nominal," Sam said.

"What the heck was that?" Jeremy's heart pounded. Thud. Thud. Thud. He didn't think it was over. He wanted it to be, but the uneasiness refused to let go.

Over the next hour, they poured through pages of code. Invisible cortical chip enhancements sped up their processing power. They were, of course, non-networked, just in case *Battlestar Galactica* was a thing and networked computers could give rise to destructive, self-improving artificial intelligence.

Gary had opted out. He liked things old-school. Jeremy never noticed the difference. He admired Gary for that, but chip enhancements were something Jeremy dreamed about since he was a kid. And he'd be lying if he didn't admit they helped with the quick thinking he needed as CEO. He just wished they'd help with his fish-out-of-the-water complex. He kept telling himself the feeling would go away, but it never did. And the more time passed, the guiltier he felt.

Sirens blared. Jeremy frowned, shaking his head. "Seriously?"

Sam's eyes widened and flicked their fingers to move the holo screen several times until the indicator showed what was happening. "Oh crap. Section seven's node's decoupled from the main ring. I don't know how."

"You want me to take care of it?" Gary asked.

"No need to get your wheels all twisted. Jeremy needs you more than I do. I'll take care of it myself. I'll go to the manual relay panel on the upper level, but I'm going to need some help with the realignment," Sam said.

"I'll send some hands from the support crew to help with the manual overrides," Jeremy added.

A large, well-lit tram connected the control room to the other sections of the array. It ran the length of each section before one had to catch the next one. The right side faced scenic windows revealing space. The forward wall housed a viewscreen with an emergency supply panel underneath and a small gold electrical panel on the left.

Sections one through ten were closest to the main control room, but there were thousands of sections, which required tens of thousands of people. The array alone housed enough people for a small city, just under fifty thousand. But despite its size, most people on the array only saw a few dozen at most since the narrow array limited the distance each person could travel.

Sam rode the tram and exchanged several segments. It handled smoothly like a quiet, first-class train cabin thanks to upgrades after the main operation's success. A short time later, the tram stopped at the final segment, and Sam hurried off in the direction of the level-two entry point.

Once there, Sam removed a section of a wall panel, revealing an attached ladder that gave access to a basement level and two upper sections. Inside, low-powered orange, purple, and blue lights illuminated the endless interior. And although circular, the distance was so great it was like walking a straight line.

A sturdy railing lined the top where Sam climbed to

find the panel. A crackle echoed through the chamber. Thin, bright white filaments erupted around the electrical panels where Sam stood and danced around their backup comms port. Sam dropped the port's plastic handle and tapped their left temple. "Jeremy. You there?" A 3D telephone image emerged, but as it did, a blue spherical orb surrounded Sam. Smaller lights extended from the orb and fluttered about, probing Sam's implant connections.

Searing pain ran through Sam's body. Every muscle fiber and bone shuddered, forcing Sam into a kneeling position on the floor before they finally blacked out.

Sam's eyelids struggled to open. As they did, painful white light forced them back down. Over the next several minutes a battle ensued between pain and the will of standing up. During the brief moments of lucidity, figures emerged in the short bursts of lights. Distant voices and chatter echoed all around Sam's immobilized body.

Sam's fist tightened, slowly at first. But as time progressed, the muscles and knuckles flexed. Soon both palms found their way face down, pushing Sam off the floor. The voices sang a bit louder. The light bled softer. And finally, the pain subsided into something approaching bearable.

"Sam. Can you hear me? The med tech is on her way. Can you hear me?" the voice said.

Sam coughed, gurgling. "I think so."

"Don't move. I've already alerted Central Command, and we're working on the realignment," the voice said, gaining more clarity with each word.

"No. Wait. Before you . . ." Sam blacked out again.

Sometime later, Sam's eyes opened. The med tech hovered above, scanning Sam's implants, pushing their head slightly left, and palming Sam's short hair in the back where Sam knew there was an odd-shaped scar.

"You gave us a good scare there for a while. How are you feeling?"

"What do you think?" Sam asked.

"Why don't you tell me?"

"I feel like a building collapsed on top of my head, and I've been lying there this whole time."

"And your eyes?" the woman asked, who still appeared fuzzy.

Sam blinked a few times, focusing on the med tech, Mirian, who had long, flowing, dark brown hair and wore a tight-fitting, subdued-red, two-piece which accentuated her slightly plump figure.

"Sore, I guess. But better than before. It was like someone was sticking needles in my eyes then moved on to the rest of my body. What the heck *was* that?"

"We were hoping you could tell us. You were standing next to the panel, but it wasn't fully open. So it's unlikely it was from an electrical short."

Sam paused for a moment. "Wait. Did they already start the realignment? I need to reprogram the panel before . . ."

Sam sat up. Tingling shot up their torso as the blood rushed down. "Whoa," Sam said, gripping the medical table.

"You can't rush this. You need to rest here the next couple of days . . ."

Sam cut her off, "Couple of days! Sorry, Doc. Not gonna happen. I have to get back to that panel and find out what's going on. If we don't realign section seven, everyone's at risk. And I can't do that until I reprogram that panel."

"Not a doc. But regardless, you're not going anywhere in

this shape. But I can relay whatever message you need back to command."

Sam sighed. Their implants were a no go. "Fine. Give me a comms channel."

Mirian tilted the embedded relay on the medical table. Sam tapped a sequence connecting them to command. "Gary. You there?"

A holo appeared, projected from the panel bottom. "Sam? Good to see you're up. You okay?"

"Still kicking. Not gonna let some computer ghost keep me down. But we've got a bigger problem. I think I might know what caused the misalignment. I hope Jeremy hasn't started the procedure yet."

A few beeps echoed from Gary's side of the comms. "Not yet. Just put the safeguards in place to prevent a breach. What's up? What are you thinking?"

Sam placed their palm down, this time easing into a more upright position mixed with a few deep breaths followed by a grimace. "Give me a moment. It'll make more sense if I show you. I'll type in the specs from the connectors," Sam said.

Meanwhile, Mirian continued with her scans. A holo listed Sam's vitals in an organized list which included heart rate, blood pressure, and a few more stats Sam didn't recognize.

The comms clicked. "I see what you mean. This complicates things. If these numbers are right, we've got our work cut out for us. And I hate to say it, but we're going to need your help."

"Sam needs to stay here," Mirian interrupted. "These vitals are all over the place."

"Listen, Doc," Sam said as Mirian frowned, "I'm not going to argue with you. I have to leave. If I don't, I could be putting everyone in danger. You know that old saying: 'The needs of the many.'"

Mirian stepped back, softening her face. "All right. I've got something for you. I usually don't give this out, since it's habit-forming, so I don't want you coming back for more. You hear me?"

Sam smiled.

"This is one and done. It's a mix of adrenaline and some uppers laced with some primitive nanos that are still in beta. You'll need to sign a waiver, just in case something goes wrong."

Tort reform was one of those things even Quinn hadn't been able to fix. "You got it, Doc," they said, signing with their finger.

"Please stop calling me Doc."

"Sorry, Doc."

Mirian injected the concoction into Sam's left arm, whose pupils immediately quivered. "Wow. That packs a punch."

"One and done. You got it? Now if you come back here, my prescription will be bed rest."

Sam gripped the seat tighter before pushing off and walking on the floor unaided. "Don't worry. I have no intention of coming back here. No offense, Doc."

Mirian smiled. "None taken, and, please, it's just Mirian."

In the control room, Jeremy continued putting out the fires from the reboot. He'd handed most alerts off to the array's communications team, but there were still a few delicate high-level interactions he needed to handle himself.

One of Jeremy's holos flashed an alert coming from the infirmary. "Sam. You okay down there?"

"Still alive, so it could be worse. Doc gave me an injection with some of those experimental nanos. And I gotta say, I'm feeling pretty good. But you should be worried about the realignment. I'm assuming Gary relayed my message. I'm heading over to the adjacent section now. Whatever caused the surge, if that's what it was, hopefully won't affect us from the flow room."

"You should have the backup you need. I've already sent over additional supporting crew to meet you both there. Let's hope we can get the array up and running again in the next few hours with no surprises. Otherwise, I'll have to tell Quinn."

"You got it. I'll keep you updated," Sam said.

What Jeremy actually thought was that he'd have to disappoint Quinn. And despite Quinn's more recent relaxed attitude, it was hard not to remember all Quinn had done and the person he'd been before.

Over the next hour in the adjacent section, Sam and Gary worked their magic to reprogram the panel at a distance. They had to manually override the already segmented system, which was no small feat. Overrides were non-networked and could only be accessed by two adjacent segments of the array. And despite all its quirks and complexity, the array still managed near-flawless execution with minimal problems, present events notwithstanding.

Sam tapped a few controls. "There. I think I've got it. But we need to go back to the panel. I'm pulling up the holo now. Let's see if we've got eyes down there."

The holo displayed both the image of the panel and the internal data it controlled within the manual relay ports. "I don't see anything unusual except for the earlier systems malfunction."

"If that's what it was," Gary said.

Sam thought for a moment. "Are you thinking someone came to this section? That should be easy enough to check."

"Or found a way to network the non-networked overrides," Gary replied.

Sam accessed the video feed from all adjacent sections and ran a motion-sensor check on the feed first before fast-forwarding through the footage. "The only thing I see over the last few days is the malfunction."

Gary stood quiet for a moment, this time on actual shoes instead of wheels. "Unless it was done before. We might need to check all the footage."

"What do you mean by all?"

"I mean all. Every station, every day since this thing has been up here. That's the only way we might learn the truth if someone's trying to cover their tracks. And not just the video footage, but access logs, if they altered the footage. Maybe even transport logs."

Sam's eyes widened. "You think it was one of *them*, someone working with Vladimir?"

Vladimir was part of the terrorist organization Quinn had originally discovered that was responsible for several terrorist attacks. That included the one leading up to the supernova which might have triggered Quinn's initial time jumping.

"I think we should be open to all angles. I mean, I don't know why they wouldn't have just sabotaged the array before the supernova if it was one of them. But who knows? And maybe it's not them. Could just be an opportunist, trying to access some free energy or something else."

Sam thought for a moment. It had been four years since they gave any serious thought to sabotage, and once the array succeeded, most terrorists faded into obscurity. But maybe Gary was right. With the message and now the malfunction, it was becoming clearer by the moment there were several missing pieces of the puzzle.

Sam closed the access lid. "Well, the good news is that I was able to reprogram the panel from here and realign the connectors. But if we have an active saboteur on board, we need to take a few precautions."

"Sounds like a plan. And while you're working on that, I'll need to pull an all-nighter to run through all the footage and message logs."

Gary was just about to head off when one of the indicators blared loudly. Sam moved their hand to open the panel. An image shot out from the inner workings of the panel. "Greetings, Earthlings," the image said.

"What the hell?" Sam said, moving back.

"Sorry. I just really wanted to say that."

"Who are—" Gary replied.

"If you're asking me a question now, I'm not synchronous, so I do apologize. I'm coming to you from . . ." The message continued. It went on for several minutes before a sudden jolt in the array disrupted the image.

Sam and Gary stood for a moment, bracing themselves for another shock. A few seconds later, Gary tapped the comms. "What's going on up there, Jeremy?"

Another jolt shook the array.

"Just putting on the final touches of the realignment. Sorry about the tremors. Should be it for now."

"Some warning would've been nice. But at least we might have the answer to what was causing the message. The shakes cut it off before it could finish, but I think we've got most of it. Sam will fill you in. I'm going to do a once-over on all our vids and system logs just to make sure we're not missing anything."

Gary finished the conversion, after which he smiled, opened his shoulder pack, and swapped out his shoes for fluorescent green skates. Gary sat lacing up until he tied his final bow.

"Don't trip and fall on your way there," Sam said.

Gary smiled and wheeled off.

CHAPTER 5

August 21, 2025, day 1, timeline 1
10:17 a.m.

THE NEXT MORNING, Cameron and Quinn arrived at the space transportation hub in Long Island. The station was the realization of what Quinn had hoped to achieve after the supernova, a celebrated spaceport hub that brought space travel to the masses.

Its main function was to transport people to the array and back, but Quinn always had a bigger vision. As the array company stationed more portable antimatter nodes, the need for local travel to the array grew, and space tourism exploded.

A buzz of activity surrounded a gigantic garden mall that fronted the entrance. It included the supernova science museum, a theme park, and alternating sections of greenery and shopping centers. The scent of cotton candy, other confectionaries, and savory meats wafted along the artistic sidewalks leading to the launch center. A few families chattered nearby as they walked by concession stands, eateries, and nearby shops.

The closer they got to the entry doors, the more apparent its monstrous size. Like the array, the transport hub was bigger on the inside than it was on the outside—technology based on exotic matter's spatial properties, which Quinn developed after watching *Doctor Who*.

The exotic matter allowed limited access to the areas between worlds in the multiverse, like extra space in a hallway, just not through any of the doors. The amount of added space depended on a multiplier of the amount of exotic matter used within a confined region.

From a distance, it took the shape of a humongous opaque egg with a launch roof roughly one-third the size of the egg itself. Two high-speed rail stations met both sides of the hub.

Inside, antimatter nodes rested on both sides of the entry point several hundred yards away. Each node spanned fifty yards and was composed of six concentric silver chrome circles which housed powerful, targeted magnetic fields. The rings performed multiple functions, including protection from catastrophic failure, antimatter activation, and energy transfer.

Large floating tubes hovered above each node, which funneled a tiny amount of antimatter like a quiet fan into the oval transport vehicles that entered a special railing above the tubes. The vehicles resembled small, sleek spacecraft, each replete with their own refillable antimatter engines. Quinn couldn't take credit for their design, but they looked like something he wished he'd created.

As they strode toward the launch area, Quinn smiled. "This still amazes me every time we come here."

A firm hand gripped Quinn's left shoulder from behind. "And why wouldn't it?" Dr. Green said.

Quinn and Cameron turned to face him. "Dad!" Cameron replied.

"It's been a while. Hasn't it? How've you been?" Quinn asked.

"Alive, thanks to you two," he said.

Dr. Green had fallen more into his role as *Back to the Future's* Doc Brown once the transport hub was fully up and running. He even looked more the part right down to the Einstein hair and shocked face with bulging eyes.

"For starters, how about setting us up in your best transport vehicle? We're headed up to the array to see Jeremy and Sam. Might as well do it in style," Quinn replied.

Dr. Green inhaled, inflating his smile to something otherworldly. "In that case, you're going to love this," he said as his white strands of hair expanded like a porcupine getting ready for an attack. "I call it Sim Infinity. It's the baddest beast I've developed yet," he said, walking them toward the direction of the vehicle.

Moments later, the vehicle inched next to them on the railing. The side hatch folded up like an oversized DeLorean but with a sleeker oval shape that had the aura of a sports car–space shuttle hybrid.

"Go ahead. Get in."

"Ladies first," Quinn said.

Cameron hopped on the driver's side and rubbed her hand along the plush, leather interior. "This is nice. You outdid yourself on this one, Dad."

Quinn entered the passenger's side and closed the door.

"Auto activate," Dr. Green said through an internal comm system.

"Do you wish to run in dual mode?" the almost human voice replied back.

"Damn straight," Cameron said. Courtesy of their implants, the transport displayed multiple specs projected on a screen only they could see.

"This baby will take you from zero to Mach 1 in a flash, so buckle up," Dr. Green added.

The inside was smooth. Manual backup panels were nearly hidden on both interior doors in the event of an emergency. The roof was transparent, allowing for ideal viewing during transport and maneuvering.

"Check this out," Dr. Green said as a joystick and added navigation controls pushed out the front panels on both sides. "Come see me again when you're both back on the ground."

They waved him off as the railing inched the vehicle higher in the tube. "Gary would love this," Quinn said.

While Quinn fiddled with the joystick, Cameron entered the coordinates and synced their flight plan to the array. "Hold on tight."

The shuttle shot over the antimatter rings, inhaling a full engine's worth before shooting them up into space. Quinn's stomach turned. "Oh. That'll take some getting used to."

The brief moment of nausea faded. A projected image displayed their progress along the projected flight path. "Docking in ninety-seven minutes," the system said.

Over the next hour and a half, they familiarized themselves with every aspect of navigation. Active navigation features were simple but limited. But Dr. Green had added special options for the Sim Infinity model. Quinn's favorite was the food synthesizer which used a combination of protein gels and flavor pastes to 3D print any food listed in the Sim database.

"You hungry?" Quinn asked.

"Could use a coffee."

"I'll take one of those too. And let's see if the burgers are any better than the models I've installed on the *Enterprise*."

Of course, Quinn had to do it. Every major aviation breakthrough had some nod to the *Star Trek* series, including his precious starship in the works. So there was no question he was going to name his first ship the *Enterprise*. And every innovation from the tricorder to the holodeck had some iteration installed. The food replicators, though, left something to be desired. Quinn was envious of Sim Infinity, even though he thought the name could use some work.

Quinn tapped the panel, which wasn't synced to implants for safety reasons. A miniature printer flashed laser-like streaks on the bottom of a ceramic plate, building up several layers in under ten seconds.

"Moment of truth," he said, bringing the printed food to his open mouth. Quinn bit then chewed slowly before he quickened his pace and swallowed a few bites. "This isn't half bad. I should get your dad's model installed on my ship. I think Jeremy would be interested in upgrading their food ports on the array too."

Cameron chomped a bite. The savory flavor triggered her taste buds. "You're right. This is pretty good," she said, scrolling through the projected images of nutritional information with her eyes. "And it's good for you too. Way to go, Dad."

Orange light flashed in front of them, warning them of the impending G-forces during the last ten minutes before docking. Over the next three minutes, the transport shuttle dropped to half its prior speed. Partial inertial dampeners activated on slowdown but took a few seconds to kick in on initialization. "That's a much smoother descent," Quinn said.

A minute before entry, systems status displayed on both the front window and implant holos. Comm notifications originating from the array flashed on the screen and directed the shuttle to the landing port.

"Quinn, we've got some news I think you're going to be interested in. We'll fill you in over dinner," Jeremy said over the comms.

"Roger that," Quinn said, proceeding to type in a few basic system requirements to allow docking to take over navigation controls.

The docking brought back memories. The array had several docking areas for each cluster of sections. And as the array company distributed more antimatter nodes, it gained more traffic. After Quinn stepped down as CEO, both off-Earth ship production and space tourism led to a rapid expansion in docking bays and port sizes. The one they arrived in was the smallest he'd seen yet.

The advantage of the smaller size was that they could fly directly into the launch bay. Pressurization was faster, which allowed for near-instantaneous entry. Once inside, array comms locked onto their implants and drew a path in midair highlighting where to go. A few minutes later, they arrived just outside the command area.

Over the next twenty minutes, Quinn and Cameron followed protocols. After a few additional systems checks and standard procedures, they made their way to Jeremy's quarters.

Jeremy had fashioned several changes to the room since Quinn vacated his old digs. Jeremy added several paintings and a few classic sci-fi movie posters which he managed to make appear more tasteful than tacky. The large window with an amazing view helped.

Jeremy's mouth opened and was about to speak before Sam beat him to the punch. "You're not going to believe what we found. And I almost died in the process."

Cameron squinted. "What!"

"Well, die might be a bit drastic, but I did find myself in the infirmary and had to take an injection of some of those experimental nanos."

Cameron and Quinn sat quietly, staring.

"Someone sent us a message," Sam said.

"What kind of message?" Quinn asked.

"The kind from the future."

CHAPTER 6

August 7, 2021, day 1, timeline 2
8:31 a.m.

QUINN LEANED OVER the balcony railing next to Cameron. The supernova's brightness had already subsided, but the interaction between the array was creating its own more colorful fireworks.

"We did it," Cameron said, eyes wide.

Quinn exhaled. "Yeah, we did." A few more moments passed. Cameron leaned closer. Quinn remained stoic, staring off in the distance, letting the silence linger.

"For someone who just saved the world, you don't seem very happy."

Quinn's brow furrowed. "There's something I need to tell you."

Cameron waited. He sensed she wanted to ask something but was still in awe of the event. Normally, she would have quipped back with something to lighten the mood while taking her best stab at the worst possible outcome. It would've been a twofer, making Quinn feel more comfortable while hinting at what most people would fear even though she wouldn't have, at least mostly.

"I've done this before."

Cameron remained silent, just looking at him as if waiting for the punchline.

"But the worst of it is, I can't remember what happened before or how I got here. The last thing I remember, we were in the future."

Quinn could tell she was still processing what he said. He gave her a bit more time before she finally spoke.

"What was the future like?" she asked.

He smiled. She knew how to break the tension, and he loved her for that. "The future's awesome. Nothing like the end of the world to put things into perspective. And everyone we know is doing great. Us included. Funny thing is, being at home here with you was the last thing I remember."

"We're still together. That's a positive sign."

"Yeah. We are, and doing amazing. The array was a massive success. I built it up even more over the first couple of years before Jeremy took over. After that, I finally got around to working on that ship that's been in my head for as long as I can remember. Almost done too. Or will be almost done four years from now."

"So you lived four years into the future? Any do-overs?"

"That's just it. None. The first year or so, I tried hard not to think about anything in the past, especially right before bed so I wouldn't accidentally end up somewhere in time before the supernova and mess things up or get stuck. But eventually, all that worrying made me think about it more."

Quinn paused before continuing. A lump formed in his throat, making it hard for him to swallow. "There were several nights where I knew I was thinking about it, dreamed about it even. A few nightmares where I undid everything. But those eventually stopped once I realized I couldn't do it anymore. And after a few years, I even tried a few times to pull a *Groundhog Day* on purpose, but still nothing. This is the first time. At least that I know of."

The sky lit up with a few more bursts of purple light followed by loud pops. She rubbed his arm. "I'm just glad things worked out."

Quinn thought about what she said. He'd almost forgotten how many times he relived days in the past and how many times he'd told her. It was nothing she wasn't already used to. And even though they both had some distance from the most recent do-over in her timeline, it wasn't exactly new. At least this time, he had some good news.

"I'm not sure what I should do. I mean I guess I should live out the day and see what happens. That makes the most sense. But I'm a little worried how I got here in the first place and even more concerned about why I can't remember. Do you think I died? Had a stroke or something?"

In many ways, Quinn already felt like an old man with all the time loops but still managed to be insecure about asking similar questions when things started over.

"I hope not. But if that's the reason, at least you get to come back and try to fix it. How's your health in the future?"

Quinn's forehead lifted, "Not bad actually. I've done enough time traveling to know I don't want my health to be the thing that gets me. And if it did, I don't think it was my lifestyle. But I guess it couldn't hurt to take a trip to the doctor. Do a few tests just to make sure."

"It may take a day or two here to book something with all the madness going on, but you definitely should. In the future, too, if you manage to get back," Cameron replied.

For the next half hour, Quinn filled Cameron in on tons of things that happened in the future. And he was glad he didn't have to worry about all that nonsense about breaking time or creating some paradox that would destroy the Earth. He just wished he could say the same about whatever it was that sent his mind back into his younger self.

Quinn suspected Cameron couldn't help but feel disconnected from Quinn's current problem. And he didn't blame her. From her perspective, he'd just saved the world. His issues were four years in the future and paled in comparison. So he let her field all the questions and calls that came in during the day to congratulate them on the array's success. He figured she'd be better equipped to respond. She told him she didn't mind, and he thought it was a good bet she was being truthful.

He took the time to load up on caffeine and do some internet recon just to make sure all was as it should be in the current timeline. A couple hours later, he switched to brainstorming different scenarios for what could've sent him back and some semi-reasonable plan of action for each case.

Around noon, they both set aside their tasks and dug into lunch. It was a habit they'd started right about that same day in the first timeline, taking a few quiet moments to show gratitude for their current blessings, appreciating all they had with present company. But by early afternoon, Quinn's brain was on fire.

"We need to call your dad."

"Surprised you haven't called already."

"I wanted to. Just needed some time to relax and think. What about you? Any ideas?"

"Your guess is as good as mine. But dad might have a few," she said.

A short time later, Quinn called Dr. Green and filled him in on his predicament. He also called Jeremy, and by dinner, his whole family was there. One by one, the whole gang arrived. Quinn's dad, Frank. His mom, Kathy. Jeremy, Sam, Gary, and a few others who might as well be family.

"Well I think it's awesome. Not only did you save the world, but now you get to go back to the future," Jeremy said.

For a moment, the comment reminded Quinn of their younger days before time fluttered it away. "Not sure that's completely true. I haven't exactly tried yet."

As the evening wore on, a majestic sunset filtered in the dining room. The interaction from the subsiding supernova and by then fully charged antimatter array added complexity to the evening sky's already deep orange-and-red hues.

Only Jeremy and Dr. Green expressed serious interest in Quinn's problem. But Quinn expected that with the culmination of all they'd just done. He listened as the evening's conversations lingered on discussions of triumph. It wasn't a bad day to repeat, saving the world and spending time with those closest to him as they reveled in their victory. He just hoped he didn't have to stay there forever, and it was a nagging thread he'd keep pulling until he found its source.

A few hours later, they had the estate to themselves. He'd enjoyed the night. It wasn't a hollow feeling, like so many of his repeats were after he'd lived them so many times. Quinn still felt connected. He didn't have to fake it, at least not yet. He just wondered if he'd feel that way again tomorrow. Or today, whichever it was.

Quinn thought about the last day he remembered in the future, talking to Jeremy on the array and holding Cameron's hand as they lay under the stars. He closed his eyes and fell asleep.

CHAPTER 7

THE ARRAY
AUGUST 21, 2025, DAY 1, TIMELINE 1
12:48 P.M.

"SO WHAT DID this message from the future say?" Quinn asked.

Sam stared at Quinn and hesitated before speaking. "We got most of the message, we think. It was interrupted in realignment."

"Realignment?" he said, pausing. "Sounds like you've been busy."

Sam traipsed toward Cameron then gave her a big squeeze. "A bit, but we're glad you both came. I've missed you. And with everything that's happened, we could use a few more eyes on things."

Jeremy typed his security codes to extend array authorization to Quinn, which Jeremy changed once Quinn stepped down as CEO. Moments later, a holo recording played the prior night's events up until Sam left to access the panel.

Once the recording stopped, Sam took over. "We think the message is from someone who's trying to help you. We're not sure with what exactly. The message was a bit vague before it cut off, but it mentioned something about the universal constant, expansion, and energy regulation. It could be something related to the array and extending its energy capabilities. And it had a sense of humor, which I think is a good sign."

Not all of the message was caught on the recording. The rest of the image and message Sam explained the best they could.

Once Sam finished, a chill swept through the room. Quinn's arm hairs popped. "You having issues with environmental controls?"

A crackling sound radiated from the nearby computer panel.

"We heard the same thing yesterday," Jeremy said.

"I think it might be related to the message. Something similar happened before I went to reprogram the access panel for realignment. Gary initially thought it might be some kind of saboteur. But I think it might just be a side effect from the message. I imagine it can't be easy sending a message into the past, or across the multiverse, depending on how you look at it. So we're thinking it needed access within our systems. The interaction might have caused some kind of malfunction," Sam added.

Quinn inhaled, processing the news. "Did you find anything that suggests someone from the ground or maybe stationed on the array had access to the systems?"

"Gary's checking on that now. He's been working on it since last night. There's still a ton of logs to pour through. And you know Gary, he's implant-free, so it might be a while longer."

The mention brought back memories from two years ago, just before the implants first gained regulatory approval.

It was the first anticipated debate since the supernova and tested the new order of things once much of humanity dropped most of the need for pretense.

Quinn expected fierce battles on both sides of the debate, but to his surprise, it simply came down to choice, with most people opting for the implants and a few others opting out. For Gary, he just didn't like the idea of a networked chip possibly providing access to someone else.

Many people expected the implants to create an unfair advantage to those with them. And while productivity increased for some, life proved more complicated. Most people fell back into their normal routines and used the excess time for other things. It mirrored the events leading up to the supernova. Some people dove deeper into their vices. Others continued living their lives mostly unchanged but with a bit more convenience. And then some maximized the implants' abilities. People in each group found their place.

On balance, the change was an improvement. A few exceptions notwithstanding, poverty, crime, and pollution continued their steady decline that stretched back decades, even before knowledge of the supernova.

"You think it might be possible to pull a *Groundhog Day*? Maybe give us a chance to get a closer look at the message and what's happening?" Jeremy asked.

Quinn locked eyes on Cameron, cuing her to speak. "He still hasn't been able to travel or loop time since the supernova."

Quinn interrupted. "Sorry, I guess I'm just back to being normal. Would be nice though. Wish I could soup up the ship I've been working on a bit more. Maybe speed up construction somehow. But looks like we're going to have to figure this one out the old-fashioned way."

Despite its advantages, Quinn didn't think he'd been too

disappointed. Time travel could be a major headache, and it had a knack for skewing one's perception of things, making even the noblest lose their way. Quinn thought maybe he'd skirted disaster, but he didn't believe he was immune, and it took a ton of effort to hold on to his nobility.

Time looping made tasks easier within the bubble, but everything else on the outside faded. The worst part was remembering people's names. Quinn lost count of how many next days there'd been where he ran into someone from two days ago who he hadn't seen in a few decades. He'd resorted to greeting everyone with, "Howzit going?" instead of calling them by name, a pernicious feedback loop that only made things worse. The irony was that one's impending demise gave added urgency and meaning to one's life. Recently, Quinn paid more attention.

Cameron took over. "So are we thinking this thing's an alien or just a fan of Marvin the Martian?"

"Honestly, it's impossible to say. From the image Gary and I saw, it looked mostly human. That doesn't mean it couldn't be alien, maybe an altered image or even some kind of physical construct. But I've told you everything we've been able to find. I'll dig into the systems a little more. Maybe it left a residue of some kind that I might be able to trace back, or at least use to hint at what kind of tech it might have employed, if that's even possible."

A few sections away from the control room, Gary sat in a large workroom he'd outfitted with advanced gaming and hacker tech. The space was originally set aside to be converted to a small port, but wasn't large enough once the engineers realized a few internal array systems passed through a central wall junction near the roof.

Port access could be tricky since it had to be synced with the array's spin cycle used for artificial gravity. And while the room was no longer designated for port use, the exotic matter used by the array to decrease needed spin created a few weak spots in the room with low G-forces. Gary highlighted the areas by retrofitting them with seats designed for immersive 4D virtual tech. The low-G gravity seats and external goggles almost gave Gary the full synth experience he lacked without an implant.

Gary inhaled the new motherboard smell from the recent installations. The scent of freshly cut computer chips, metal, and rubber all melded into an aroma soup that triggered the familiar endorphin rush whenever he enjoyed either a gaming or long workout session.

Gary sat in one of his chair mods sifting through security holo footage embedded in his latest role-playing game creation. The only downside was the game was limited to one section of the station at a time due to array protocols. He didn't have anyone else to fight against, so he played against a program he designed to mimic himself but with added unpredictability.

He streamed the footage at triple speed, running one type of image scan from the gaming console to pick up anything he might have missed. The combination increased his speed beyond what an implant could do. Then a half hour in, he realized he could increase the through rate further by creating multiple avatars and layering different tasks for each one.

For the past eleven hours, he found nothing suspicious. And as time ticked on, his focus shifted from the potential spy on board to each subsequent game level. But in parallel with the game, the added digital copies of himself labored in the background analyzing increasingly difficult possibilities of tampering he'd programmed them to inspect. And just as he was about to finish the hardest level yet, one he'd yet to crack, alarm bells sounded.

He'd rigged the alerts to activate in full sensory mode: moisture, temperature, pressure, smell, and, of course, audiovisual. They all hit at once. From high atop a virtual cliff, the game forced his avatar into a dive toward an endless chasm. The wind speed increased. Lights flashed around from all directions. Water from a nearby waterfall streamed toward him, with droplets smacking his face and neck hard. Ephemeral ghost demons and dinosaurs lunged at him from either side.

The game was malfunctioning. Once the system picked up a preprogrammed cue and sounded the initial alarm, it was supposed to exit into basic mode. "Exit," he said. The game continued. His pulse jumped. "Exit," he repeated. Nothing. The game continued. He dove further down the chasm into increasing darkness. Light faded completely into pitch black, but the noise grew louder, almost to the point of white noise, but then a familiar crackle echoed in the darkness.

"Exit," he tried again. Still nothing. He kept racing down in pitch black, but the noises shifted, some familiar, others so foreign he couldn't place them. Occasional branches from the nearby waterfall grazed his arms to the point of discomfort, something that shouldn't be possible with programmed game settings.

His pressure gloves came outfitted with a backup kill switch that he never used. It was a crude, incomplete connection that, when used, would require a full reboot. Half the time, he'd lose the full data bank from each session, so he'd never used it after beta testing.

A dull red light emerged in the darkness as his avatar

dove further, but by that point, his brain couldn't distinguish between the game and the outside. He dove further. A ragged gray mass expanded in the center of the red light, which grew in intensity as he continued his accelerated fall.

The mass took on texture, and before long, a full picture emerged of jagged boulders surrounded by a streaming lava pit. Gary's speed increased. The stones' razor-sharp protrusions were nearly upon him, and just as they were about to meet his face, he pressed the fail-safe.

Instantly, the scene shifted. Ambient light increased, but he was still inside of a game construct. He lifted his game visor, revealing the workroom he expected to see. Gary ran a systems check on the gaming console and double-checked segmented networking connections just to see if they had been tampered with. When he couldn't find anything, he lowered his visor and reentered basic mode within the construct.

The crackling sound returned. Gary expected another image to appear, perhaps the same figure from the night before, but only the basic construct remained. He designed it to look freakishly large with indistinct boundaries, and a few feet ahead of him were 3D images of readouts filtering in from the irregularities pulled from the processed system logs and holo feed.

"This can't be right," he said.

The holo recording displayed inconsistent and fluttering time stamps. They were there one moment and gone the next. The contradictions spanned nine months' worth of recordings.

He homed in on a different section, but each time, the holos changed the second time he ran them. The variability continued regardless of which section within the time frame he inspected.

"What are you trying to tell me?" he asked.

Crackle. "Great question, and I'm glad you've finally asked."

Gary shot back. He attempted to lift his visor but was unable to. The slide mechanism remained immobile, as if jammed.

"What the heck? Is someone out there?" he said, unable to see outside the construct.

"It's just you, and me. Or I. I can never figure that one out," the voice said.

"Who are you? What do you want?"

"Sorry. This message is designed to auto reply to only one question at a time. I will start with the first one. 'Who am I?' Well, for starters, a better question is 'Who are we?' And the answer to that question is something you'll have to discover on your own," the message said.

Gary rotated his head, eyeing both sides within the construct, but still spotted nothing. "Don't mess with me. Where are you hiding?" Gary tightened his fists.

The voice interrupted, "To answer the next question: 'What do we want?' Well, that's why we're here. There's only one way to find some of the answers you're looking for, but you won't find all of them. I wouldn't want to give away our advantage. If you want to find the answer to the first question, you'll first have to beat the game," the voice said.

"Whoever you are, I have no intentions of playing this game of yours, but I am going to find out who . . ."

The voice cut him off, "Oh, and I forgot to mention, I've analyzed your systems and have initiated an antimatter cascade failure which will occur if you're not successful in solving the question. You have exactly seven minutes and thirty-two seconds to solve the problem. Good luck! Well, not really. But if I were you, I wouldn't let that stop you," the voice said.

CHAPTER 8

August 8, 2021, Day 1, Timeline 2
8:33 a.m.

QUINN SAT AT the dining table palming his mug of hot coffee. He'd been sitting there for over an hour ruminating over the possibilities and racking his brain trying to remember what happened after the conversation with Jeremy in 2025.

A short while later, Cameron strolled up behind him and placed her arms on his shoulders, rubbing them a few seconds before she pulled out a chair and sat next to him. "So which timeline is this?" she asked.

He was about to say, "The wrong one," before he stopped himself. "It didn't work. I tried to do my thing. You know, thinking about the last day I remembered in the future right before I fell asleep, but nothing. Maybe it's the same reason I couldn't loop time after the supernova in the first timeline. I'm thinking maybe I used up all the residual juice from the dark matter or that there was a hard fork in the multiverse before and after the supernova."

"From what you told me about the future, would that be so bad?"

Quinn's heart sank. The possibility that he'd have to repeat the next four years hit him all at once. He wondered if it was like waiting for lightning to strike twice. Things definitely broke his way in the future, but any number of factors could change that, not least of which was whatever shot him back into the past. It felt like the opposite problem of when he first discovered time travel. Instead of needing to go back in the past, he wanted to move in the other direction.

"The last time this happened, at least I could loop time. If I'm not able to do that, I'm not sure I have many options," he replied.

"Did you try that yet, looping time?"

"Actually, no. I just tried to wake up back in the future. But you're right. I'll see if I can wake up this morning again tomorrow, and if that doesn't work, I'll try to repeat yesterday morning. And if that doesn't work, I'll keep trying something else," he said.

Cameron smiled. "That's the spirit. Now that we've got that out of the way, we've got this pesky little problem of the biggest parade of all time planned for you in Times Square. And it may be *your* second time, but I'm not about to miss this. So let's hop in that helicopter of yours and fly our way over there."

Flying a helicopter was one of those skills he'd picked up along the way when looping time prior to the supernova. He thought it would come more in handy than ice sculpting. And at least his flying skills were still sharp, though most of the time in the future it was flying spaceship simulations.

A short while later, they arrived at Quinn's heliport above the estate. The copter was small and black with red markings. Cameron sat in the copilot's seat, being a pilot herself. Quinn put on his helmet, checked the equipment, and then kicked the propellers into high gear before liftoff.

The first time they left for the parade she did the flying. He'd been so high strung on whether or not the array would succeed. And even though he wasn't in the driver's seat last time, he was still too much in his head from the event and in no mental shape to pilot an aircraft.

Quinn flew higher. Eventually, he eyed the area where they'd break ground on the launch center. It was only a couple years in the future, but felt so far away. He was glad he'd already preprogrammed the coordinates into the copter since the terrain was so different than he'd recently remembered.

As they closed in on the city, enormous crowds gathered like a colony of ants swarming toward a few free morsels of food.

Once he turned the bend beyond the Trade Center, gigantic balloons clogged the main arteries of Manhattan. There was one balloon of the array, two of the Twin Towers, which were still standing in that universe, and a host of others that represented different Hail Mary projects and leaders of projects prior to the supernova.

Quinn neared their landing coordinates and did his best not to get too distracted by the scene. The initial crowds he saw exploded into a spectacle of epic proportions, and even more clusters of balloons became visible, inspiring and lighthearted designs that more accurately depicted the moment.

He'd never seen such a huge crowd. He'd attended numerous celebrations and gatherings in his time, but this made them all appear minuscule in comparison. It was as if every soul in the greater New York area had come out that night and then multiplied themselves by ten.

Cameron led him toward the back entrance of where they'd housed the parade float. It reminded him of how some of the media and politicians berated the parade planners leading up to the event. They argued that it was insensitive and took away focus from trying to save the planet and would be all for naught if the human race failed. But Jeremy shut most of them down by funding the entire celebration himself.

"There he is," Jeremy shouted over the roaring crowd as Quinn made his way onto the float.

Quinn couldn't help but smile, feeling as if someone had plucked him from his living room sofa and dropped him into the movie *Ferris Bueller's Day Off*. And he took that movie's lessons to heart, one of the most important being that dancing spreads joy.

Seeing the world come close to destruction so many times made him take to heart the ephemeral nature of life and how so many people misunderstood both risk and life itself. Much of what society argued was important was both subjective and contradictory. He realized that it wasn't just life that needed protecting, but the celebration of life.

What was the point in being alive if you couldn't allow yourself to enjoy it? And the irony was, a healthy dose of celebration did a lot more for the physical and mental health of society than all the PSAs and government mandates ever could. And most times, the latter did the opposite.

Quinn climbed to the top of the float next to Jeremy and breathed in the night air. The sights around him made him forget his current dilemma. That moment was what life was all about, the reflection, the celebration, the gratitude.

Jeremy spoke over the crowd. "There were a few moments there where I wasn't sure if you'd do it."

"If *we'd* do it," Quinn added.

Jeremy smiled and let the smile grow unabated before chuckling. "You might be right. But you did most of the work."

Quinn said nothing about the latest predicament, not wanting to spoil the moment. "But look what *you* did. This is amazing," Quinn said, remembering how the first time he was too much in a daze to enjoy it.

The celebration forced them both to shout. But Quinn wasn't complaining. He was, however, amazed at the sheer magnitude of every aspect of the parade.

"How did you get all this confetti?"

"Oh, that? Nothing a few confetti cannons and airplane drops couldn't handle."

Quinn realized he hadn't seen that side of Jeremy in a while. Once Quinn stepped down as CEO, he hadn't seen any of Jeremy, for that matter, much less his lighthearted self.

"So what else have you got going on with this thing?"

"You mean the parade? Well, you've done this before. Haven't you?"

"Yeah, but just humor me."

Jeremy smiled and put his arm around Quinn, pointing left. "Over there, you can see the big hat on the Statue of Liberty's head. If we were closer, you'd see the surrounding boats and ferries around the island. There's over half a million people surrounding her alone. And the hat was a gift from the French," he said.

Quinn was surprised he missed it while flying over. A large black puffy hat easily half her size donned the statue's head. A gold loop, apparently mimicking the array, graced the center of the hat decorated with blue-and-white jewels, which he assumed were stars.

Then Jeremy pointed right. "And if you look close

enough in the direction of Central Park, you'll see a few bubbles, nontoxic and biodegradable, of course. Wouldn't want to damage the trees. We've got the biggest foam party on the planet ever!" he shouted, throwing his arms up in the air and attempting a few awkward dance moves.

Jeremy prattled on for the next several minutes detailing every over-the-top aspect he'd planned. All the while, hordes of people of all ages and walks of life danced alongside them. Young couples danced amongst themselves, older retirees strode next to them, even families with kids, all walking in unison in the direction of the float and rest of the parade that was slowly making its way down Manhattan Island.

Security kept most people off the float, but every so often a few wild participants managed to hop on and dance a bit, most of them poorly before they were gently escorted off. Even security got in on the action, throwing in a few moves with some of the people a few seconds before they kicked them off.

The madness continued unabated for hours, only growing in intensity as time passed. Normally, Quinn may have become concerned with the intensity of the celebration, but he didn't remember any major problems the first time, not that he was paying close attention. For a brief while, he forgot about his plan and allowed himself the moment.

Quinn tried to enjoy the rest of the event, but the more he thought about it, the less clear his recollection of the night in the first timeline became. He didn't remember when he went home, what time he went to bed, or barely anything else from that night. It was almost like a traumatic experience where someone blocks out most of the surrounding events.

His focus shifted back to his thoughts on trying to repeat the day. But he wasn't sure if it was already too late. It was well past midnight, and on all the occasions when he'd looped time, it had always been before the next day.

Despite his agenda, the parade showed no signs of letting up, and there was no feasible way to maneuver past the crowd or find his way back to the heliport in the Financial District. A few more hours ticked by, and as dawn broke, the crowds thinned just enough where they could make an attempt to move. It took some effort, but a while later, Quinn and the rest of the gang might make their way back near the Twin Towers.

"This was something else. I had a great time, at least for the first half of the night," Quinn said. But the cause of his backward time jump was a dangling thread still begging to be pulled, and he'd already missed one more night.

The crew went their separate ways, with Quinn and Cameron dodging the still plentiful crowd. Just as Quinn was about to enter the building that housed the helipad, a vaguely familiar figure caught his eye from across the street.

A man with heavily furrowed skin and a scraggly beard glared at Quinn with eyes like knives that pierced Quinn's soul. A filthy grin draped across his face before he ducked into the shadows and disappeared from view.

Cameron lightly tugged on Quinn's arm toward the direction of the building, and he turned his attention to flying home. This was the moment he dreaded.

"You think you might want to fly this thing back?"

"Sorry. I've had a couple, so that honor goes to you."

Quinn glanced back at the shadow, half expecting that man to reappear, but only a few tipsy pedestrians hobbled into view.

He continued forward, lugging his uncooperative legs

toward the elevator. A short time later, he boarded the copter and flew back home.

Quinn fought fatigue and felt guilty about it the entire flight. He'd made an effort to limit stupid behavior, and flying while half asleep wasn't exactly smart. He made a mental note never to do it again if it could be avoided. Of course, if he needed to save the world, all bets were off the table.

A short time later, they made it safely home. Quinn crashed on the bed and gave up the idea of waking up yesterday, at least until later that evening.

Sometime early in the afternoon, Dr. Green arrived in the lab at Quinn's estate. Dr. Green's hair wasn't completely gray yet. It was just his short beard and a few streaks that went up both sides. He'd just recently stopped dying his hair, but Quinn could see it in his eyes and the lines in his face he hadn't yet given himself permission to fully let go.

"It's still bothering me. I'm going to keep trying, but I'm not sure it will do much good," Quinn said.

Dr. Green's blank expression did little to comfort him. "Give it some time. There's no rush that I can see. I know you seem to be in a hurry to get back, but the future's not all that far away."

"Maybe so," Quinn said, not believing it for a moment. On the surface, things were great. He couldn't deny that, but he thought if he didn't pursue the mystery, at some point he would regret it. "But we should be prepared in case things go south. Just look what happened last time."

Quinn could tell Dr. Green's head was thinking, working through different scenarios. "Given the limits of what we know, I can think of two choices that have a higher probability than most. The first that comes to mind is that you died and you're in a time loop, a long one. You may have to live out the next four years for near infinity or until there's some kind of conflagration of timelines, at which point, things could get messy."

Quinn thought about that for a moment. It could be worse, at least until the end. Four years was enough time to at least live, but it still would put a damper on things. "And the second option?"

Dr. Green sighed. "Could be another catastrophic event of some kind. Maybe related to the supernova in some way. The array could've malfunctioned, destroying the planet, perhaps deliberately. Or it could be some effect of the supernova we didn't account for, a second pulse of some kind that got delayed in interstellar space, a deflection of a newly created accretion disk from the supernova remnants."

Quinn sulked. His face warmed, and he considered the daunting task of piecing together the puzzle.

"But there could be a more innocuous answer. Maybe you got hit in the head or got drunk and just don't remember what happened. In a fleeting moment, your mind reflected on the past, and the holographic universe sent your consciousness back one more time. It could be that you need to recreate the exact circumstances that brought you back. And if that's the case, I may know a few people who would be willing to give you a good whack."

Dr. Green's humor usually fell flat, but it was a valiant effort. "I think I'll pass on that," Quinn said.

They discussed more possibilities, each one more remote, and eventually, Quinn was satisfied with the discussion. He was convinced he'd either died or the array had exploded. That's despite the near impossibility based on the design and built-in safeguards. In either case, he would have died.

And that would make the most sense as to why he was sent back to just after the first supernova. The more he thought about it, the more he became convinced that a new explosion would have given him the same time-hopping abilities as before, unlike an ordinary death.

The only remaining question in Quinn's mind was why it didn't work when he tried to go back. Eventually, he concluded that the nature of the latest catastrophe only let him repeat time from the beginning of the new timeline. He was likely stuck in the current one, only able to relive days he'd lived in the new version of the timeline.

He put his theory to the test, reflecting back on the moment he noticed his presence a couple days ago. He imagined it, reflected on every aspect of it from his wife's soft hands to the supernova's waves of white light, and then he closed his eyes.

CHAPTER 9

The Array, August 21, 2025, day 1, timeline 1
1:11 p.m.

GARY ATTEMPTED TO tear his visor off, but it was still stuck in place. He smacked the fail-safe on his wrist a couple more times, but each attempt failed.

"The clock is ticking," the voice said.

Gary gritted his teeth. "Where are you?"

"And if you're asking me another question right now, you won't get a response until you successfully complete all the tasks, starting with these."

The construct stripped out most of the bells and whistles, displaying instead a few connected screens with data flow and mechanical schematics Gary recognized as parts of the array. Gary didn't move. He just inhaled a few slow breaths.

"Tick tock. Tick tock," the voice said.

A giant rectangular digital clock resembling immense game clocks in a basketball court appeared on a solid wall in front of him.

"Every thirty seconds, you get a shock. And each shock

will become more unbearable until . . . ," he said pausing, "kablooey."

A few more screens appeared; now there were six in total. The additional screens he didn't recognize, but he could tell the patterns were related to energy flow conduits used to transfer antimatter between array nodes.

A few beads of sweat trickled down his forehead and a few more seconds ticked by, but he remained immobile.

"Task number one," a different voice said. It was more digital than the voice that had been speaking to him earlier.

The scent of ozone filtered into the construct, and Gary felt his chair shoot up from the ground. One screen expanded in front of him.

"Erase all records you've found in the last twelve hours. For this task, you have exactly seventeen seconds."

"You can't be serious. There's no way I can do that."

Gary remained motionless, refusing to budge or touch the screen. The wall clock continued to tick down. It was divided into two sections. The side on the left displayed the time until cascade failure at seven minutes ten seconds, and the right side showed the time left remaining for each task. In the center was a smaller inlet that counted down from thirty seconds, and it was already down to nine.

"I'm not doing this," he said as he continued to wait out the time. Each second struck louder. The wind within the construct increased, and the ozone odor grew more intense, like just after the start of a heavy summer downpour. Three. Two. One.

A bolt appeared from the clock and lunged toward him, zapping him on the head and then flowing down the rest of his body.

"Enough of this nonsense," he said, still shaking in pain.

His fingers catapulted onto the modified holo keypad. He pulled one file and swiped left, opening the encoded contents. He pounded away and responded, pulling another file. The holo screen flashed to black, and then lines of code flowed down the screen. One file after another, he emptied the contents.

He couldn't tell if the hacker knew what he was doing, but he was going to draw out as much time as he possibly could until he did.

"That's it," the voice said. "Keep going."

Gary wondered if the command center had any idea what was happening. But based on what the message told him, his guess was no. He chose to risk it. This person or thing needed him, and that meant the worst it could do was hurt him. But if it killed him, Gary wouldn't be able to do what it needed. It was possible it might try to manipulate Sam, but Sam didn't have a fully functional game system set up the way he did. It could still try crude methods to control anyone on the array, maybe through their implants. But if that was the case, why hadn't it tried that already?

Gary continued with the charade, emptying out digital folders and making it look as if he was destroying the code. What the messenger didn't see, or at least what Gary hoped it didn't see, was the shadow copy he made with each file emptied.

Like some master hackers, Gary invented his own modified code. Encrypted systems and network connections required a backbone language, but Gary added an additional layer through a modified environment. While one might expect another expert to anticipate that extra layer of environment, Gary had created it in such a way to blend in with the existing background code.

The clock ticked to zero, and another shock jolted into

Gary's chest. Saliva spilled from his mouth as he briefly lost consciousness. A few moments later, he came to with twenty seconds remaining till the next one.

"Hey, man. I finished your task."

This time, the voice didn't reply, but the clock kept ticking. The task list removed the file deletion, so Gary assumed his plan was working, but the next task would be hard if not impossible to fake. The task was to network the computer nodes between array segments, something protocols didn't allow and the array's hardware was designed specifically to prevent.

Gary went to work, this time doing something completely unrelated, working on building one of his avatar duplicates within his game program but in such a way that it might mimic networking the nodes.

Another shock jolted him from his chair and singed his trunk. He collapsed forward, and for a moment, his heart stopped, skipping three beats before quickly restarting.

So far, the messenger proved correct. Each subsequent shock became more debilitating, and each time he came to, Gary wondered how the heck anyone could be expected to think quickly in those kinds of conditions.

Then a thought came to him. Gary had so far kept his avatars non-networked specifically for this kind of eventuality, some rogue hacker or computer system working against the array. And while he wasn't too worried about his avatars turning into Skynet, he was much more concerned about networked segments creating a critical failure, sending enough antimatter through nodes to wipe out the sun.

It should be possible to begin working on networking pathways but prioritize the connections to subroutines that would network his various avatars. By the time he needed to switch over to the segments, he could activate preprogrammed routines to make it appear as if the functions would network the segments, when in reality, they would be working on a signal to send to the rest of the array and shut down other critical functions.

He could create a microsecond surface connection that would send enough juice to trigger the final fail-safe. The array would lose substantial power, but whatever nefarious reasons the messenger needed a network array would be stopped dead in their tracks.

Gary continued with his plan, thinking about what message to send and how to encode and unpack the encryption to avoid detection by the messenger. Then Gary realized something. He'd been working on the assumption that the messages from the other evening and the hacker that was controlling his system were from the same person. In fact, he started to think that it was possible, even likely, that all three messages came from different people, related perhaps, but different.

Array protocols included several emergency responder beacons that personnel could activate in various ways, but one of the simpler safety measures was a couple of low-tech communication tools they'd modified from basic Morse code. One of them was a simple burst of either sound or light in three slow bursts followed by a one-second pause and four quick bursts. Gary thought the command would be simple enough to route to the command center in multiple ways if needed.

The tougher part was finding a way to bridge the segments and transfer enough of a jolt to activate automatic array safety measures to shut down the systems. The only way he could think of involved using the magnetic coils to force an electrical current to bleed through adjacent segments. If he could get enough juice.

"We've detected deception. You won't succeed," the voice said, this time in a creepy synthetic tone.

Gary ignored the voice, keeping his eyes peeled to the holo screen and typing away code to execute his command. Two successive jolts shot into Gary. The second forced him to blackout for ten seconds. When he came to, he typed in the final commands and hoped it would work.

The entire time, he'd been working to find what was keeping his visor held in place. It was a crude bit of code that used a combination of electrical and chemical compounds in his skin to keep it clamped shut. "Almost there," he said.

"Your attempts to elude us will fail."

Static crackled within the construct. Gary was nearly done, working several routes simultaneously. If he could steal a few more lines of code without the messenger noticing, he could link external magnetic coils. The trick was power.

While the array stored enough energy in the form of antimatter, the magnetic field and exotic matter held it in stasis, preventing it from interacting with normal matter. They could hold only a small reservoir at a time that flowed through segmented pools using exotic matter. That meant the most a saboteur could access was one small pool.

The problem was, that single pool was all someone needed if they managed to succeed in getting it. The energy could rip apart entire segments of the planet. If accessed, it could also send the array careening into Earth.

To avoid such an eventuality, it took a monumental effort to briefly access a single pool of antimatter. Quinn designed the array allowing only limited electrical current to flow through all systems not part of antimatter storage. This included systems designed to access the bridge networks to tap into the stored energy.

Access had to be piecemeal. There were emergency release valves from each node that could tap into a tiny amount of antimatter in case array energy stores were depleted, but those were tiny, molded into place by the supernova event using exotic matter.

Regardless, all safety measures and designs couldn't stop someone from causing some type of damage if they were motivated. And unfortunately, that applied to just about everything else on the planet and in space.

"You will fail," the voice said.

"Let's see if you can stop me," Gary replied.

A moment later, Gary secured access to the magnetic rings. His fingers whipped back and forth executing commands. In a matter of seconds, he activated the emergency signal and triggered a full systems shutdown.

"It's not going to work," the voice said.

Gary responded by finally tossing off the visor and decoupling the restraints which held him in the mod chair. He hurried to backup communication walkies, which he didn't ever think he'd use, and explained to Jeremy what had happened.

In the main control room, lights flashed and sirens wailed. Jeremy and Sam bolted to their stations, and Quinn joined them on a nearby panel.

"The magnetic coils from section seven are about to collapse. We're going to need to accelerate shutdown somehow to prevent a blowout," Sam said.

Jeremy scanned the holo in what looked like an attempt to find a possible solution.

"I have an idea," Quinn replied. "If we can force access to section eight by draining all energy from external systems, we could gain access to emergency reserves from adjacent sections. That would force safety measures to decouple the coils from nearby exotic matter rings. Computer backups would detect the secondary protocol and jump forward sixty seconds on the shutdown."

"But there's a big problem with that," Sam interrupted. "If we do that, we risk blowing two sections instead of one. Depending on how much access that thing has had to our systems, it might be possible it could find its way into both rings and do twice as much damage."

"You have a better idea?" Quinn said.

Sam stood for a moment, brow furrowed and unresponsive.

"What about you, Jeremy?"

From the look on his face, Quinn could tell Jeremy felt overwhelmed, which Quinn thought was odd considering how he handled himself since he came on board. Jeremy acted as if he was sure of himself, happy even. But in that moment, Quinn thought the emergency had uncovered the illusion Jeremy appeared to have worked hard to pull off.

"No? Well it's your call. But I don't think we have much of a choice," Quinn said.

Sam waited for Jeremy to signal authorization.

"Fine. Do it."

Sam's hands were lightning quick. "Rerouting reserve conduits now," they said.

Jeremy straightened, moving into position and typing in commands. "Something's blocking the connection to the relays. The signals aren't being sent."

"Hold on a second. I'll see if I can't maneuver a workaround. This messenger might know most of our systems, but I've still got a few tricks up my sleeve," Sam said.

"While you work on the relays, I could work to empty out

section nine manually. I don't think I can do both sections, but I might be able to shut down one, keep the damage down to one section maximum if we're not able to stop the overload," Quinn said.

"If you're not able to shut it down, you won't make it out of there. You sure you want to risk it?"

Quinn didn't hesitate. "I've already lived more than enough lifetimes. You know how much damage this could cause if we don't shut this down. Just don't hold back on my account. Hopefully I'll return before you two finish."

They both gave him a look of approval. He pulled out a portable jumper about the size of a motorcycle. Engineers fashioned it after one. Quinn could sit and lean forward or back like he was cruising on a Harley, but the engine was magnetic. Designers took the idea of a hoverboard run by magnetic strips that lined hallways and rooms in the occupied section of the array's outer ring.

Quinn zipped to section eight in a tenth of the time a tram would take him. When he arrived, he began opening conduits on the outside panel connecting a barrier room between the two sections. He'd need to get inside the section and manually deplete power using an energy rod designed to reroute excess energy to empty space. It would essentially convert the power to a stream of excited electrons that the rod would propel through empty space.

If Quinn was quick enough, he might be able to finish the job before the shutdown and zip over to section seven to assist Gary and repeat the process in case Sam failed. Only time would tell.

CHAPTER 10

Date and location unknown. Timeline unknown. 9:37 a.m.

QUINN RUBBED HIS eyes and looked again just to be sure he'd read the driver's license correctly: Frank Black. It didn't change. "This can't be right. What day is it?" he asked, still staring at the license.

"What do you mean? It's Saturday," she said, stepping closer.

He slid back. "I mean the year. What year is it?"

She crinkled her forehead. "What do you mean? You know what year it is."

Quinn guessed it must have been sometime in the '80s. And he couldn't believe he hadn't recognized her before, but she looked so much younger, and with the hairdo, she was like a different person. "Please, just tell me. What year?"

"It's 1984."

Quinn's eyes widened. He thought about what he would tell her. *Hi, Mom?* Maybe, *I'm not really your husband. I'm your son.* Or, *I'm actually your son from the future, and somehow my mind got switched with Dad's mind in the past.*

Where was Frank's mind anyway? The situation didn't make any sense and didn't match with how he thought time travel worked. He'd never really answered the question of where the other mind went, but just assumed it continued in new branches in the multiverse. *If* he swapped out his consciousness.

"This isn't right," Quinn said, wanting to say more. Then he remembered Jeremy's seven rules of time travel. They'd both broken them so many times, and it was only a matter of time before it came back to bite him if he kept breaking them. The most critical time was always on the first jump before he'd established the new limits or whether he could even travel back.

"What isn't right? You've been acting weird all morning," Kathy, his mom, said.

She moved closer to him and placed her hand on his shoulder. She softened her eyes. "Are you angry with me? I know things have been tight lately, but you know we really needed this trip. Or is that it? Are you upset about me pushing you to take the trip?"

Quinn sighed. His head hurt, considering what he could say that didn't make him sound completely insane or like a total tool. He knew by that time his parents had already been married for a while. So maybe they could weather a bit of a rough spot if the situation went sideways.

Quinn then realized he hadn't been born yet. He did the math in his head. "Oh, snap!"

"What? What is it?"

"I think I'm going to be sick, really sick this time," he said, running back into the bathroom and slamming the door.

Quinn flipped up the commode lid and emptied his breakfast into the porcelain bowl. He wiped his mouth then washed his face, running the water into his hands and letting the water cool his heated skin. He fiddled with the towel, drying his face, then inspected his reflection.

He fondled his face, running his fingers down from his brow to his lips, discovering how much he resembled his dad at that age. The eyes were a bit different, the irises' gray flecks didn't pop the way his did. Next, he moved on to his chin, then his ears, and finally the back of his head. The shape felt wrong, more square in the back, less oval shaped. The hair texture was rough and thin.

He heard Kathy approach the door. He stepped back, dabbing his face one last time with the towel. "I'm not sure anymore. I think maybe we should go back, see a doctor or something."

He could hear the air deflate from her lungs. And he knew they didn't get out much, especially when he was younger. This might have been their first trip in years.

He opened the door. "I'm sorry. I really am. I know how much you wanted this. Anyway, no. I'm not upset. I think it's just food poisoning, and I'm not thinking straight."

He could see her processing what he said, unsure if she bought it. At least now there was some evidence he'd just flushed down the toilet. And he knew she didn't suspect he was her time-traveling son from the future, but he needed to consider how to navigate the rest of the day and how to get back home, if that was even possible.

Over the next several hours, he pieced together what he could by scavenging through his belongings while trying to avoid appearing like a lunatic. He scraped together ticket stubs and discovered he was somewhere in the Florida Keys. Based on the math, he also concluded last night was likely the day he was conceived.

He had a tough time convincing her not to take him to the hospital. It was a fine line not appearing too sick but just enough to cancel their trip and return home. They had just two more days on the trip, the only three-day weekend they'd probably had in a long time.

A few hours later, they found themselves at the Key West airport hunting down a flight back to New York. "Are you sure you don't want to go to a hospital? We're already here, and it would save on the tickets we'd have to buy for the return trip."

He didn't want to think how much they'd need to pay to change the flight or the cost of the hospital visit. "I think it might cost more if we go to the clinic. I'm not feeling great, not feeling good at all. Head's not on right, and I just want it to stop spinning."

That much was true at least, but next week would be worse. Quinn didn't have a clue about his dad's job other than he got a new one a few years later. If only he'd jumped a few years later he might have been able to pull it off.

A short time later, they adjusted their flights and boarded. Once they were buckled in their seats, Quinn attempted to devise a game plan.

The passengers directly in front of them puffed away on their cancer sticks, forcing billows of cigarette smoke to waft in their direction. He briefly considered asking them to put them out due to his fake illness. Instead, he spent the next two hours analyzing his options.

By the end of the flight, he thought he had a well-devised plan. He'd attempt to travel back to the future that night. If it didn't work, he'd try the following day. If that didn't work, he'd call in sick from work for the next week. During his time off, he'd visit a clinic and claim he had amnesia. The downside was that it would likely get him laid off from his job. He would do everything he could to prevent that from happening and even began planning for that eventuality as well. His dad was the easy part. Handling his mom would be a different story.

Arriving to a home Quinn had never seen was jarring. He knew they'd moved to the burbs just before he was born, so seeing his parents' tiny home in the city was surreal. He could understand why they wanted to leave. His parents were both from the area, but met in the city when they were younger and looking for work.

As he walked into the building and fumbled for his keys, he sensed eyes staring at him. Kathy put her hand on his lower back, which made him feel worse.

They lived in a run-down area near Central Park. A humid, musty odor hung in the air. The discolored walls and paint-chipped corners told the story despite the new drapes and decent furniture. The bathroom pipes squeaked, and so did most everything else.

Later that evening, Quinn convinced Kathy he needed to sleep on the sofa despite her prodding. He wasn't sure if he could think about the future and travel back, being in his dad's body, but he had to try it and keep doing it until something worked.

He reflected on the last moment he remembered, staring up at the stars underneath the night sky with Cameron. As he did, a few flashes he didn't recognize entered his mind. He attempted to hold onto them and study their meaning, but the fragments vanished and created uneasiness in his thoughts. After a few more tries, he gave up and resumed thinking about the picnic blanket, the call with Jeremy, and the comfortable life he'd made for himself in 2025. He closed his eyes and fell asleep.

September 2, 1984, Day 1, Frank's body
8:42 a.m.

Quinn woke to Kathy sitting next to him, stroking his forehead.

"How are you feeling?"

Quinn sighed, realizing it might take a while to learn what happened and find a solution, if there was one.

"I think I should go to the clinic. Why don't you stay here, get some rest? Make the most of our alone time," he said, feeling dirty just for saying it.

"But it's just us the next couple of days. I want to spend them with you."

"That's my point. I don't want you wasting your day in a waiting room. I'm the one not feeling well. I'm not dying. Just some food poisoning, maybe a bad stomach flu or something. I don't want you wasting your free time, the little you've had, over this."

After a bit more convincing, she agreed.

A short while after Quinn left, Kathy called her mother, Etna. "Something's wrong with Frank. He's been acting strange the last couple of days. We left the Keys early because he said he was sick, but something doesn't feel right."

Etna's long black hair overwhelmed her petite frame. She sat in an uncomfortable position at her study in her spacious Queens residence. The home had a sleek, well-kept modern interior that suggested an income above their class.

"What do you mean by strange?" Etna asked, holding the phone upright, revealing her inked wrist adorned with celestial bodies.

"I can't put my finger on it. He's just acting differently, and I get the feeling he's lying to me."

"About being sick?"

"I thought so at first, but I did hear him toss his cookies back in the Keys. Just not sure about now. He was insistent on going to the clinic after we got back, but didn't want anything to do with it before we left. But it's more than that."

Etna considered what her baby said, at least still a baby in her eyes. "I never thought Frank was rotten, but sometimes those worms get sneaky, good at hidin'. Hold on a sec, honey," she said, putting her hand over the speaker. "Hey, Marty, why don't you get in here? Kathy's on the phone."

Marty hurried in from the other room, still quick on his feet but with a few more lines under his eyes than one might expect. Marty shared the phone as they both listened. "What is it, darlin'?" he asked.

"Was just telling mom Frank's acting strange. I think he's hiding something."

"Want me to find out? If he is, I got no problem kickin' his ass. No one messes with my little girl."

Etna could hear Kathy exhaling. "No. Don't do anything. Not yet anyway. It just doesn't feel right is all. Just thought you might have some advice."

"If you really want, we could hire a PI. Put a tail on 'em. If you want me to, just say the word," Marty said.

"Please don't. Let's just see how this plays out. I might just be blowing this thing all out of proportion."

"Then maybe try talking to him. Couldn't hurt," he replied.

"But if he gets squirmy, you let us know. Best to cut this stuff off at the legs before it eats away the rest of the body," Etna added.

Quinn strolled into the clinic, deciding it would be best to lay the groundwork and report amnesia. If he waited until later, it would be hard to make another excuse to explain away. He completed the paperwork and sat for twenty minutes before the doctor called him in. At least wait times were shorter in 1984 than in 2025, but in fairness, they had improved over the prior few years.

A midfifties doctor with a Tom Selleck mustache and the name tag Abrams approached. "Mr. Black?" the doctor asked.

"I guess that's me," Quinn said, and followed the doctor into his office. Inside, several dated posters hung on the wall describing various venereal diseases.

"So tell me a little more about what's happening."

Quinn squirmed, choosing his lies carefully. "I don't remember anything before yesterday. I woke up in Key West next to a woman who's apparently my wife. I managed to convince her to go back home. At least I'm assuming that's my home, hoping it might ring some bells."

Dr. Abrams stood quietly, inspecting Quinn's face and using a stethoscope to listen to his heart. "Do you know if you drank any alcohol recently, maybe took something the night before?"

"The only thing I remember drinking was coffee and water, and maybe some tea at lunch."

The doctor ran a few standard physical inspections and asked some additional questions which Quinn assumed were to discover if he was drugged out or a lune. Then Quinn gave him a brief rundown of his time after waking up the day before and how he managed to make it back without telling Kathy the truth.

"Is there anything else? Maybe something you don't want to share for whatever reason?"

Yes. I'm a time traveler from the future in my dad's body. The amnesia part is real. I just don't want you to think I'm a total nutjob. Of course he couldn't say *that*. "No, that's it," was all he replied.

"You mind if we take a few tests and if I call in someone who specializes in this sort of thing?"

Quinn assumed the specialist would be a shrink. The blood work might actually do him some good, but the other might present a problem. He knew from his history that it would be a few more months before major changes in mental health treatment. Before then, it would be much easier to find himself locked up somewhere if he didn't tread carefully.

He complied with the blood work and spent the time deliberating answers to potential questions, most of which he expected they probably wouldn't ask. A short while later, an older lady with the name tag Whitlock who reminded Quinn of Dr. Ruth stepped into the room as Dr. Abrams stepped out.

"So where do you live? Frank is it?"

"Nearby, close to the park."

"And do you remember this?"

"No. Not really. It's just where my wife took us when I got off the plane. I told her I wasn't feeling well, wasn't thinking straight. That much is true. But I've never seen the inside of my apartment, at least that I can remember, until I walked in there with her."

"And what *do* you remember?"

"I already told the other doctor this."

"I know. Let's just go through this one more time. It'll help us sort out things."

Quinn ran through the list, being as truthful as possible and sticking to the bare minimum of what he needed to say with no embellishments, just leaving out the time-traveling, mind-hopping part.

"You seem like a reasonable man, Frank. Do you know what kind of work you do? Are you employed?"

Frank rummaged through his wallet and displayed a pay stub, showing it to the doctor. "I'm assuming I work at this place, and it's recent, so I'm guessing that's where I work. But I don't recognize the name, and I'm not sure what kind of work it is."

"And you mentioned you're married. Is that right?"

"Yeah. That's right. Her name's Kathy. That much I discovered on my own."

"And why isn't Kathy with you right now?"

Quinn had thought about that question, feeling a bit more confident he might actually pull it off. "I knew something was wrong. I told her I wasn't thinking straight. But I was scared. I thought she might get angry, think I was lying. Maybe after I went to the doctor, it might be easier. She might believe me."

"Let's talk more about that. Do you get scared a lot, worried maybe someone's out to get you?"

He knew where that line of questioning was going. "No. Nothing like that."

"Do you know for sure? I mean, if you don't remember anything before yesterday morning, isn't it possible you do?"

"That sounds like a trick question."

"I'm not trying to trick you, just getting a sense of what's happening."

"Like I said, I can't remember what happened before. I'm not sure how else to answer."

"I'll just come out and ask you, Frank. Are you being completely truthful? Is it possible you came here with ulterior motives, maybe committed a crime and need an alibi for the crime, a cheating tryst, or something?"

"I don't think you're doing your job very well, Doc. If I was a criminal, do you think I would come out and tell you? And if I were crazy, do you think I would tell you that either?"

"There's no need to get angry, Mr. Black. And I don't like to use that word. I work with a lot of patients who have mental health issues, but I've also seen many patients who, for whatever reason, feel the need to lie. What I'm trying to figure out is which one you are."

"Why do I have to be either? Isn't it possible I could have some physical condition, maybe a blood clot or something, or a brain tumor? I haven't even had an MRI."

Quinn got the suspicious feeling Dr. Abrams and Whitlock already made up their minds, and he didn't like where this was going. He started eyeing the exit, estimating how long it would take him before he could get out safely if he managed to evade security. The clinic was small, so he didn't think they had more than one guard, and he doubted they were used to that sort of thing. But the clinic could be a target for addicts, so it might be possible they had more security than was visible.

"Why don't we just wait for the blood work to come back. How long is that going to take?"

"Listen, just calm down, Mr. Black."

Quinn noted the switch to last names. He wanted to say he was calm but figured that was like an alcoholic saying they weren't an alcoholic.

"Why don't you call my wife."

"So you're sure she's your wife?"

"That's what she'll tell you when you call. She knows

I'm here. She's expecting me back soon. She knows I'm not feeling well."

"Okay, Mr. Black. Let's do that. What's your wife's number?"

Quinn realized he had no idea. "Give me a second. I'm not sure exactly, but I might have it somewhere in my wallet."

"Don't you think if you knew you had amnesia you might check first to make sure you had your wife's number before you left?"

She had a point. He should've looked it up in the phone book, if it was even listed. "Can you call information? Or do you have a phone book nearby?" he asked, still sorting through the small pieces of paper in his wallet.

He'd forgotten how much paper people needed to keep and crap people had to remember before cell phones.

"It's going to be okay, Mr. Black. We'll get to the bottom of this. If you have a wife, I'm sure we'll find her."

"You don't need to handle me. Just call 411 for Pete's sake."

Quinn felt the walls closing in, almost as if he was already locked up. And he could tell from her mannerisms, he'd need to act fast, get her off balance then bolt out the door.

"No one's trying to handle you. I just want you to be safe. We want everyone to be safe."

The situation and the word "safe" made Quinn sick to his stomach again. It wasn't that he was opposed to safety. He wanted security just like the next person. It's just that whenever someone in authority was completely clueless or had an idea they wanted to shove down someone's throat, it often came back to safety.

"I just want to get back to my wife," he said, suddenly realizing his next move. "I found it. Here's her number," he said, handing her a small piece of paper with tiny writing. It had a few numbers, but no telephone numbers, and they were small enough that she'd have to spend a few seconds inspecting them before realizing it was a dupe.

"Okay, Mr. Black. We'll give this number a call," she said without looking too closely.

"I'll be right back. I just remembered something," he said, lying. As soon as he was out the door, he bolted. He figured the clinic didn't have enough to hold him or call someone after him. He just needed to make it back to his apartment.

Once he arrived on the street, he hurried across the block and ducked into a nearby clothing store. He debated on whether to wait, buy something as a disguise, or hail down the nearest taxi. He chose to hide in the store and waited a few minutes, then scoped out the scene before exiting.

The clothing store carried a hodgepodge of music video nightmare outfits in bright contrasting colors. Puffy leather jackets and tops with bulbous shoulder pads littered the clothing racks. There were so many it was easy to hide, and he had enough cash to buy something reasonably cheap and escape in a taxi, assuming they hadn't spotted him.

He waited another twenty minutes for good measure before buying the cheapest outfit he could find to disappear into a crowd. He put a few bills on the counter, took the change, and eyed the street through the glass before stepping outside.

Dozens of women walked by wearing an assortment of velour and synthetic fabrics, several in sheer stockings and tailored suits with bulging shoulder pads. Others wore baggy harem pants with clashing animal prints and puffy sleeves.

Once he felt secure enough, he exited and attempted to

hail a taxi. Two occupied cars drove past him before he spotted an empty one that slowed down as it approached. Just before he got in, a couple of men came running out toward him from the direction of the clinic.

The cab stopped. "Columbia University, and I'm in a hurry," Quinn told the Pakistani driver.

The taxi drove off. The reflection of the two men throwing up their hands appeared in the rearview mirror. He figured the driver assumed they were trying to hail the cab and missed. Quinn then saw the men jotting down something on a notepad, which he assumed was a license plate.

Quinn inhaled a few breaths. "So you work at Columbia?" the driver asked.

"No. Just have some business up there with my wife's father." He was about to say more but opted for less so it couldn't be used against him. The clinic might have called the cops already.

A few minutes later, Quinn noticed a couple of police cars half a block away. "You think you could step on it a bit?"

The driver shifted in the seat and adjusted the rearview mirror. "Everything all right?"

"Just in a hurry. The lab closes soon. Want to get there before it closes," Quinn said.

The driver glanced at Quinn in the rearview. "You should be all right. I know several people from there, and it stays open pretty late."

"Yeah, but he's leaving early today, so I need to get there before 3:30." Quinn glanced in the right wing-mirror, spotting the squad car one car ahead of its last position. He debated having the taxi take the next right. If the cops planned on stopping him, they probably would have already turned on their sirens. But it was possible the shrink told them about the situation, and they didn't want to tip their hand. In which case, they'd simply follow until Quinn stopped.

"Can you take a left on 109th Street? I'll book it from there."

"It'll take you longer to walk from there."

"That's fine," he said, figuring he could lose the cops in one of the nearby pastry shops. It might be best to circle back and lay low. The only question was whether he'd go back home or do something else. He could always head back to Columbia the next day. Or at least he hoped he could. Maybe he'd need to get Kathy to clear things up with the cops before he did that.

A few minutes later, the taxi pulled over. Quinn got out and ducked into one of the nearby shops. A few street performers did their thing at a nearby intersection, providing cover for him to scope out the scene.

It was the Michael Jackson impersonator who drew the largest crowd, something he'd expect to see closer to Midtown or Broadway. The guy was slick and even had an uncanny resemblance with perfected moves he hadn't seen in a while.

After Quinn was satisfied the cops were gone, he dug into a bear claw and chugged down a twenty-ounce coffee. He considered his plan some more and chose to hunt for a nearby hotel to stay in for the night. If the police came looking for him, it might keep him from finding Dr. Green. And if they managed to take him to the hospital, he wasn't sure if they'd stuff him full of drugs and mess him up even more than he already was.

A few minutes past four, Quinn strode in the opposite direction of Columbia wearing a shaggy hat and long jacket. He clambered from the Upper Eastside toward Midtown, looking right away from the street when cops rolled by.

An hour later, Quinn found himself at the police station

in a questioning room, which brought back memories of his first few time loops before he saved the world.

"So. Frank is it? I heard you gave the clinic quite a scare, threatened a couple of doctors then busted your way out of there," one of the serious-looking male cops said.

Quinn checked their badge numbers, just to be sure he wasn't talking to Scott Channing's father, who Quinn knew from the original timeline. "That's not what happened. I'm sure you can check the cameras for that."

The cops chuckled, looking at each other. The thin cop with sideburns a decade out of fashion smiled. The hefty one did all the talking. "That clinic ain't got no fancy cameras. You should know that. Or maybe you shouldn't since they're sayin' you ain't right in the head. And it's obvious you ain't right in the head, 'cause who wears a frickin' long jacket in early September. Where do you think you are, Vancouver?"

"I like Vancouver," Quinn replied.

"Looks like we got a wise guy here," the cop said in a thick New York accent.

"So tell us what you were doing at the clinic? Trying to score some morphine? Couldn't find your supply of H. Is that what it was? You look a bit scrawny and got tired eyes. Maybe haven't got much sleep in a while?"

"Lawyer," Quinn said. "Not saying another word until I talk to my lawyer."

The pudgy cop smiled. "No problem. Just tell me your lawyer's name and number, and I'll be sure to call him."

"Call my wife. She knows the number."

"What's your wife's number?" the pudgy cop asked.

Quinn said nothing.

"Like I said. Wise guy. Sorry, pal, but if you don't know the number, I can't help you," the serious-looking cop added.

"You got a phone book?" he said, hoping to get lucky this time. He knew he at least got a phone call. "And a quarter," he added.

The cops made a few jokes at Quinn's expense before taking him to a free phone with a phone book. He scanned the last names until he located his mother's number.

"Kathy," he said, wanting to say "Mom," "you have no idea how good it is to hear your voice. I'm at the police station. I'll explain later. I went to the clinic, but they thought I was nuts. I almost didn't get out of there. Can you pick me up?"

A short while later, she picked him up, not saying anything until they sat in the car.

"What's going on with you? It's like I woke up married to a different person."

"That's not too far from the truth," he said.

She took her eyes off the road a second and stared at him. "What's that supposed to mean?"

Quinn sighed. "I told you, I haven't been feeling good. But what I didn't tell you is that I've been having trouble remembering things."

She stared at him with a confused look on her face. "What kind of things?"

"Everything. I remember you, but that's about it. I don't remember anything about us, just vaguely your face. I don't remember our apartment, my job, any of my friends. Just you, your parents, and my parents. That's it."

"Is this a joke? Because if it is, it isn't funny."

He had heard that familiar phrase so many times, and it had worn thin in his mind. But he wasn't about to tell her the truth. At least not yet. And that meant he either needed to get to Dr. Green or find out how to travel back or forward in time. Dr. Green was the most viable option.

"I'm not being funny. You can come with me to the clinic if you like. You think I'd make up something like this? The cops told you themselves. I need to see somebody, someone who might be able to help me."

"I thought you said you only remembered me and our parents."

"That's true, and a few other people. I swear. That's the truth."

"The truth keeps changing. What else haven't you told me? Are you having an affair? Is this some elaborate excuse to cover something up? Because I'm racking my brain, and I can't think of anything. None of this makes any sense."

At that moment, Quinn wanted to quit. He wanted to give up on everything he'd done before and just let it go. He'd saved the world, saved the people he cared about, and done everything right. But in that moment, he felt like he hadn't gotten anywhere. All he had to show for it was an angry mother/wife, a near trip to the psych ward, and a replay of decades-old fashion with no internet.

A few hours later, he resigned for the evening, allowing both himself and Kathy to cool off while he reflected on his next course of action. And whatever happened, he was going to pay a visit to Dr. Green.

He spent the last half hour before bed memorizing his address book and scanning the *Wall Street Journal*, just in case. He made his way to bed, focused hard on what he remembered from earlier in the morning just after he woke up, and closed his eyes.

CHAPTER 11

Sᴇᴘᴛᴇᴍʙᴇʀ 2, 1984, ᴅᴀʏ 2, Fʀᴀɴᴋ's ʙᴏᴅʏ
8:42 ᴀ.ᴍ.

QUINN WOKE TO Kathy sitting next to him, stroking his forehead.

"How are you feeling?"

"Oh, yes!" he shouted.

"What? What is it? Does that mean you're feeling better?"

Quinn smiled. "Halfway there anyway."

Quinn beamed. It felt like an oppressive weight was just lifted. He might be stuck in the past and in his father's body, but at least he could loop time. He considered whether or not to tell her, then decided to speak with Dr. Green first, just in case the situation was permanent. He hadn't worked out how he was going to navigate handling his mom if he had to stay there for any length of time.

"Want to check out a matinee then maybe a show?" he asked.

She smiled. He knew his parents hardly ever went to movies, and he never remembered seeing a Broadway show, which was a shame.

After she tried to steer him toward *The Woman in Red*, he managed to convince her to see *The Adventures of Buckaroo Banzai Across the 8th Dimension*, which felt more like his life at the moment.

They had exactly two hours until the movie, and he chose to save meeting Dr. Green until the next today, assuming he could loop the day again. If not, he'd take one for the team and go tomorrow. But after his near miss before the first loop, he needed the day off.

He made scrambled eggs and fruit, figuring he'd lay off the bacon in case she asked about his stomach. After breakfast, they kicked back on the sofa, and he scanned through the Sunday-morning news, catching up on a few pieces of information he might find useful at some later point.

Quinn made a point of writing a few key days and stock ticker symbols he'd burned into his brain in 2021 after looping back into his high school body. When he was in the throes of preparing for the array, he memorized a few key stock trades for every year a few decades earlier just in case they ever came in handy. He also studied a few events, natural disasters, sports games, elections, all on the off chance he got stuck in the past.

"When was the last time we saw a movie?" he asked, figuring he better start catching up on some recent history he'd missed out on.

She thought for a while. "I can't remember. It's been so long."

"I'm sorry about Key West," he said.

She inched closer. He could tell she wanted to kiss him. "Um. But I'm still not completely better. I'll see what we've got in the medicine cabinet. Better take something with us just in case."

Her face dropped. "If you're still not feeling better, you sure we should be spending most of the day out? Maybe you should stop by the clinic."

"I'll pass on that. Really, I'm much better, just not a hundred percent," he said before escaping to the bathroom and sitting down on the toilet.

A short while later, he shuffled back to the couch and buried his head in all the magazines they had scattered on the table. He'd never gotten to enjoy the magazine culture before the internet nearly wiped it out. Quinn settled quietly into the pages and dove into the material until it was time to leave.

When they made it to the movie theatre, he let himself relax. He took in the theatre vibe, which was more authentic than he remembered in the future. Movie posters from recent movies, *Red Dawn*, *The Karate Kid*, *Revenge of the Nerds*, and *Ghostbusters*, all lined the walls near concessions.

He bought the largest box of popcorn, buttered with real coconut oil before they replaced it with the crappy substitute. He added Goobers, Bon Bons, and a red slushy to wash it down.

"You sure we can eat all that?"

"Gonna try," he said, leading her to the fifth row from the front, dead center.

Throughout the movie, he gobbled down the popcorn but took it easy on the Goobers. The slushy they'd devoured halfway through the movie, but he took the time to refill it the moment Kathy got a little too close for comfort and tried to lean on his shoulder. He could tell she was already getting suspicious of his questionably timed exits.

Despite the awkwardness, the movie was great. He'd seen it a couple of times, but not quite as many as some of the others that were still showing.

They'd selected *Cats* for the Broadway show, and it didn't disappoint. They ate a light meal afterward and made it back to their apartment before ten.

The evening was tricky to navigate. He still made his best attempt to avoid all physical contact, which she made more difficult with her constant overtures. His excuse was overdoing it on the popcorn and snacks during the movie, for which he got roundly scolded. He made a note to be sure to repeat it again in the next do-over. He still had a few movies he wanted to watch on the big screen at least a dozen times each.

Around eleven at night, he made his way to bed, focused hard on what he remembered from earlier in the morning just after he woke up and closed his eyes.

September 2, 1984, day 3, Frank's body
8:42 a.m.

Quinn woke to Kathy sitting next to him, stroking his forehead.

"How are you feeling?"

He grinned, almost too much but not quite exposing his teeth. "I've got an idea," he said.

He convinced her to see *Ghostbusters*. It wasn't *Groundhog Day*, but it would do. They made it to the theater, a different one this time. He'd figured if he was going to loop time, he was going to make it as unique as possible. He didn't have any pressing concerns except getting back into his own body and chose to have a little fun with it along the way. He was just with his mom instead of Cameron.

He repeated the process over the course of fourteen loops, thinking two weeks was long enough for a vacation.

He'd managed to get through all the movies from the movie posters he'd seen in the first two theaters, plus a few more he regretted. Each time, he pulled the same shenanigans with his mom, ordering too much food and stepping out to refill his drink. After the first couple of times, he got smaller and smaller amounts of food so he could go back a couple of trips.

But like all his other time loops, things could get old fast if he didn't have a purpose. And despite how much fun 1984 might have been, he still wanted to be in his own body back in the future.

September 2, 1984, day 16, Frank's body
8:42 a.m.

Quinn woke to Kathy sitting next to him, stroking his forehead.

"How are you feeling?"

Quinn gave a half-hearted smile, already preparing himself for the long slog. "A little better. I think I should stop by the clinic this morning just in case, but I don't want to waste the rest of the day. We should see a show tonight. What do you think?"

Kathy smiled and nodded in approval.

"I'll take a taxi and breakfast and call you from a payphone if I need anything," he said.

He chose to skip the clinic and head over to Columbia to see if he could find Dr. Green. He thought he could call in a few sick days if he wanted or needed to go a few more days forward, best to limit any permanent damage to a minimum just on the off chance he found himself stuck.

He'd already started laying down the groundwork, looking for a brokerage account to open and checking their bank accounts. His parents had a measly $1,482. His dad made a little over $300 after taxes, but they had a rent-stabilized apartment at a ridiculously low $204. He figured if he needed, he could take out a couple hundred and put it back before Kathy noticed, if it came to that.

Shortly after ten, he made his way to Columbia. He had to ask around for directions to the main office, where he found a campus directory. He knew where the Data Science Institute was located, but that didn't launch until 2012, so it took some time to navigate until he found Dr. Green's office.

Dr. Green stood immersed in drawing chalk equations on the board. Papers cluttered his large office table, and several clunky computers sat in the back.

"Dr. Green. You don't know me, but I have some information I know you'll find intriguing. And I think we can both help each other."

The youthful Dr. Green wrinkled his eyes in an annoyed look. "I'm busy. Can you come back tomorrow?"

"Trust me," Quinn said, still raising his voice outside the glass door while tapping. He looked in both directions just to make sure he was out of earshot of anyone who might be walking nearby. "You're going to want to hear what I have to say. I know you're working with a team, and one of your colleagues is doing something illegal, something that could end your career."

"I don't have time for games. I'm busy doing real work here. Can't you people understand that?" he said, still immersed in the equations.

"No games. Just give me a couple minutes, and then I'll leave."

Dr. Green said nothing, still writing equations on the board. Quinn stood a few more minutes, waiting for Dr.

Green to acknowledge his presence. A few people walked past him in the halls. Quinn waited for the walkway to clear.

"I need to talk to you. This is serious."

Dr. Green tapped the board with his chalk. "Serious? What is serious? Some would say the universal constant is serious or that time is serious. But is anything truly serious? Isn't seriousness just a societal construct, all subjective based on our current whims and the latest impressions based on various stimuli?"

"You might be right, Dr. Green. I don't doubt that for a second, but your wife may have other ideas."

Dr. Green turned, squinting. "Who are you, and what do you want?"

"Let me in, and I'll tell you."

Several more people walked by. Quinn stood quietly while Dr. Green added a few more flourishes on his equations before opening the door.

Quinn cleared off a seat covered in papers. Dr. Green returned to the chalkboard, ignoring Quinn's presence, at least from what Quinn could tell. "What if I told you that time travel was real?"

Dr. Green continued working another half minute before replying. "I'd say tell me something I don't already know. Einstein showed us how it's possible. And time dilation is a fact of everyday life. Say something new."

"What if I told you I'm from the future?"

Dr. Green stopped and turned. "I'd say you still haven't answered my question. Who are you, and what do you want? As you can see, I'm busy here, and I don't like people wasting my time."

"My name's Quinn. Quinn Black. I know your wife because I'm married to your daughter."

"I don't have a daughter, Mr. Black."

"You will in the future. I'm from 2025. I've traveled back in time before, but this time I have a problem."

Quinn waited in silence and could tell Dr. Green was considering what he'd said. "I can see you have a problem. My guess is you're either on drugs or playing some stupid prank that I don't have time for. I'm a busy man. I have important people that are very demanding waiting on me, and when people like you waste my time, they don't like it. So why don't you just leave, Mr. Black?"

"I'm not leaving. And I can prove I'm from the future."

"You've got twenty seconds before I call campus security."

Quinn explained what he knew about the Russian involvement with Dr. Green's project and how Dr. Green often used the project's credit card to buy incidentals but would promptly pay it back, and that it was his sloppy accounting that was going to get him booted from the project and visited by the government once things went south.

Dr. Green turned toward Quinn and squinted. "Who sent you? I know you're not from the future, but you clearly know a lot about me. Are you some kind of investigator? Maybe someone working for a rival project?"

"I told you, I'm from the future. So I know how this is going to play out. You've still got time to stop doing what you're doing, but I need your help. Something's not right, and I don't know how to fix it."

Dr. Green put the chalk down and sat at the table next to Quinn, giving him his undivided attention. "And why should I believe you're from the future?"

"You just said you believe in time travel. That is the math you're working on right now, isn't it? Variations on M-theory? So I know you know it's possible."

"Possible, yes. Likely? Well that's a different story. And even less likely is that idea that someone manages to travel back through time to tell me."

Quinn thought about his response. He needed some engagement before Dr. Green humored him. There wasn't enough traffic to pull a *Groundhog Day* without cooperation from Dr. Green himself. "It's time travel, but with a twist. I don't believe in paradoxes. And I know you don't either. But in the future, a supernova explosion nearly destroyed the planet. I was thrown back the morning of the explosion and then realized I could go back even further with my mind."

Dr. Green's eyes told Quinn he was intrigued. He went on to explain the entire situation, right down to the most recent wrinkle of being thrown back into his father's mind.

"And let's say I believed you, which I don't. What then? Why do you think I can help you?"

"Truthfully, I don't know if you can help me. I don't know why I got thrown back this time. I don't remember the exact circumstances. But you're all I've got. I figure we can help each other. I can tell you more about what I know about these men on your team, do some recon, maybe loop time a bit, engage them to throw them off, and travel back a few days if things don't go as planned. I don't see any downside for you."

"The downside, Mr. Black, is that I think you're full of it. You think I'm stupid because my brain works differently than most people's. You think because I may not talk the same way or act the same way or care the same way as other people that you can take advantage of me, get me to spill some kind of secret that I'm not supposed to. What I think is that you're trying to get me sacked or maybe testing me to see what happens. For all I know, you could be working for my boss."

"Well if that's the case, then you're already screwed, because I just told you about the accounting issue. That's enough to get you canned alone, if not prosecuted if someone really wanted to."

Dr. Green pounded his fist on the table. "Leave! I want you to leave right now."

CHAPTER 12

SEPTEMBER 2, 1984, DAY 16, FRANK'S BODY
11:46 A.M.

IN DR. GREEN'S lab at Columbia, Quinn walked away, using the evening to replay the conversation in his head and consider a different approach.

Over the next ten loops, Quinn followed the same strategy but with different conversations, gathering tiny bits of information from each one in the hopes of building a narrative Dr. Green could buy to give Quinn an opening. Day after day, loop after loop, Quinn kept at it until he found his opening.

SEPTEMBER 2, 1984, DAY 26, FRANK'S BODY
11:47 A.M.

"So you see, I think this could benefit both of us. Just have lunch with me, and I can prove it," Quinn said.

Dr. Green agreed. Quinn drove with him via taxi to a busy cafe near Times Square. Quinn pulled out a pad and pencil and ticked off a list of a dozen random events that he knew he couldn't pull off with anyone's help.

The first loop was a bust. But on the second time, he got Dr. Green's attention. It still wasn't until the fifth try that Quinn convinced him, and they went back to the lab.

September 2, 1984, day 31, Frank's body
1:13 p.m.

Dr. Green closed the blinds in his lab. "So where do we start?"

"I need all the names on your team. We'll keep looping today because I don't want to go too far into the future for the same reason I told you before."

"You mean your job?"

"Yeah. That. It will take some navigating, and I figure we should try to solve this before then. And of course, there's the issue of my mother. A bit awkward, don't you think?"

Dr. Green hesitated for a moment. "I think I know why you came back here, or at least part of the answer to how you came back here."

Quinn waited for him to say something, but he never finished the train of thought. "So what is it?"

"Your conception. It's likely the time loop is limited to your existence. In which case, you came back to the moment of conception."

Quinn thought for a moment, realizing he didn't have a clear memory of waking up in Key West. His first recollection was staring straight ahead at the blank wall of the hotel like in a trance, and then for some reason, he just snapped out of it. "I think you might be right. This time was different. But that still doesn't explain why or how I'm in my father's body."

"That I haven't figured out yet."

"Do you think I might be stuck in it?"

"If you did it the first time, it stands to reason you might be able to do it again, though in the opposite direction. But that isn't always the case, as with entropy. So the short answer is I don't know."

Dr. Green continued on. They blathered about different theories of time travel and the holographic universe, coming up with a few off-the-wall theories that were more speculation than having any basis in fact. For each potential thread, Dr. Green drew up a series of equations and Quinn jotted down notes, not knowing how long it would take him to recreate the math, so he had Dr. Green keep it as simple as possible so they could start each loop with at least a basic possibility.

By the end of the evening, they had six different theories. Quinn memorized the first primary set of equations with the intent of spending a full day on each one in the next loop.

During the next six loops, Quinn and Dr. Green spent the full day exploring the possibility of each theory to the extent time allowed, and each time they didn't get any further. Quinn spent a week on each theory and repeated the process until complete.

Seven weeks later, Quinn and Dr. Green hadn't come any closer to resolving the question of how or why Quinn had gotten thrown into his father's body or what might have happened to get him thrown back, aside from what they'd already speculated.

September 2, 1984, day 80, Frank's body
1:13 p.m.

"We haven't gotten anywhere with the math, so I think we should split up. You work on the theory you think is most promising, and I'll scope out your colleague," Quinn said.

Dr. Green wrote all the information he had and the usual patterns for the colleague, and Quinn laid out the details of the equation.

"At some point, I'm going to have to wake up tomorrow. I'm just hoping we make more progress with your colleague than we've been having with the equations."

Dr. Green acknowledged Quinn's math then dove deep into the chalkboard. Quinn left the research lab then hopped in a taxi to find a place to stake out the colleague.

An hour and a half later, Quinn spotted Dr. Green's colleague, Saad, a young Saudi with terrorist ties, and waited patiently for something interesting to happen.

During the next four hours, Quinn sat across the street with a pair of binoculars peering into Saad's window. He couldn't tell much of what was happening on the inside, but he was able to see that Saad was alone and no one else had come in or out of the Hell's Kitchen apartment. Around 5:30 p.m., two rough-looking thugs, one whom he guessed was Russian and the other Middle Eastern, possibly Southern European, entered the hallway.

Quinn captured their license plates along with the make and model of the car, which was a dark-colored, old, rusted Jeep. A few minutes later, they entered the room and spoke with Saad briefly before all three left and approached the Jeep. Quinn managed to hail a taxi before they left.

It was the same friendly Pakistani driver as before. "It's a nice evening, isn't it?"

"Please, follow that Jeep," Quinn replied.

Quinn inspected the two men in the back closely. Saad was with the Russian. They talked the entire time and didn't have anything with them. Whatever they were doing, Quinn assumed it was at another location. What he needed was a way to listen in on their conversation.

September 2, 1984, day 81, Frank's body
5:33 p.m.

Quinn waited at a nearby cafe, this time on the same side of the street. He carried a walkie-talkie (which he called a "walkie"), since cell phones were out of the question, but he didn't get the opportunity to use it, at least not yet. He also wore unassuming early September clothes with tacky colors that blended in with the rest of the 1984 outfits on the street.

He had precisely three minutes to place the listening devices in the Jeep. And once they left the apartment, he'd plant the other device there, where Saad would return in a couple of hours.

Once Quinn spotted them, he jumped into action, but just as he was about to plant the bug, a cop spotted him. He was on the younger side, in his early thirties, and still in decent shape. His face hadn't fully hardened like the cop standing next to him, who looked like he was straight out of *Terminator 2*.

"Hey. You there. Stop right there. What are you doing?" the officer asked.

Quinn complied. As the officer approached, he recognized the familiar 732 badge. "You're kidding me, right? Let me guess. Officer Channing?"

"Keep your hands where I can see them. No games. And I don't care if we've met before. I see a lot of perps on the street," the officer said. "So tell me, how is it that you think you know me?"

"I know your wife," Quinn said, instantly wishing he could take it back.

"Now you listen to me, you little son of a bitch. I don't know what kind of business you're trying to pull here, but you're not doing yourself any favors."

"I'm sorry. That's not what I meant. If I told you the truth, you wouldn't believe me."

Officer Mark Channing furrowed his brow. "You *don't* know me. Do you? I've never seen you before. I'm good with faces, and I think I would have recognized a blockhead like yours. You got some ID, mister?"

"Black. It's Quinn, but my ID says Frank."

"Okay Quinn-Frank, hand it over. And no funny stuff."

Quinn delivered the license. Officer Channing inspected it, and Quinn's mind lit up with possibilities. It was too much of a coincidence. Had he been assigned to that beat for a reason, maybe offering cover in case someone got too close to the apartment?

The officers called in the license, and a couple minutes later returned with a quick stride. For a moment, Quinn thought they realized he was the guy who'd evaded the cops after slipping out of the clinic, but then he remembered that hadn't happened in the current loop.

"Put your hands behind your back. We're taking you in."

"On what charge?"

"Breaking and entering. That's what you were doing, wasn't it? Breaking into this car?"

"I was just walking by. I fell down. That's all. It's not a crime to fall down, is it?"

The expression on his face told Quinn that Officer Channing didn't believe a word of what he was saying.

September 2, 1984, day 82, Frank's body
5:33 p.m.

Quinn waited on the same side of the street but this time at a different cafe. He spotted Officer Channing staking out the apartment in his patrol car, out of view from Quinn's prior locations. He wondered how long they'd been watching the apartment and decided he'd stop by earlier in the next loop, and he'd have a backup in case they were still there.

Quinn met up with Dr. Green later in the evening and filled him in on the situation. He explained how he was thinking Officer Channing was covering for the goons and that there was more going on with them than he expected.

"I'm starting to think this may not be the same timeline. Or if it is, someone's been making changes. I don't remember anything about Mark Channing working with your colleagues," Quinn said.

"That doesn't mean it didn't happen in the last timeline. Maybe you're just uncovering it now. I think that's the more likely scenario. And are you sure that's even what's happening?"

Quinn considered it, still not sure if that were true. "How's your progress coming along? Did you find anything with the equations?"

Dr. Green frowned. "I think you should be working on this. Maybe I should be the one tracking down the rest of the team. It may take you a bit longer, but at least you won't forget everything with each loop."

Quinn's physics was solid since he developed the array in numerous loops, but his focus was more on material sciences and less about time travel, though the two weren't unrelated. He thought it would take substantially longer, although it wasn't a terrible idea. It just might take him longer than he'd hoped.

He'd already tried moving back to the future and even going back several days before, but the only days he could loop were after the switch. He began to think he would be stuck there for years, so he gave himself a work schedule, five loops on and two loops off.

Over the next four weeks' worth of loops, Quinn and Dr. Green managed to discover that one of Dr. Green's colleagues was in fact part of the group connected to several terrorist attacks in the future. From the recon in his colleague's apartment, they also learned he'd been a member since he'd joined the team and was likely a plant from the person who funded the research at Columbia.

SEPTEMBER 2, 1984, DAY 110, FRANK'S BODY
7:32 A.M.

Officer Mark Channing smacked the alarm buzzer in his modest Brooklyn home. He inspected his wife lying asleep beside him. She was out cold, motionless. He reflected on their days together before things began to fall apart.

He slid off the bed, and after a shower and meager breakfast, he waited outside in a small shed in the yard. Shortly after 8:30 a.m., a tall middle-aged man entered the shed and locked the door behind him. He was balding, with deep furrows in the center of his forehead, a long scar from his left ear to his jaw, and scruff on his chin with a mix of blond and gray splotches.

The man positioned himself near Mr. Channing. "I've been watching you very closely, Mr. Channing. And I think you know you haven't done everything I've asked," he said in a thick Russian accent.

"I've done everything you've asked. And I swear she doesn't know anything about it. No one does. But you have to keep your end of the bargain. You promised if I did what you said, you'd leave them alone."

"I know you pride yourself on trying to be a good husband and father. I know you love this pathetic little country of yours with all its platitudes about freedom and whatnot. But let me tell you, it's all just meaningless tripe. None of it matters. Nothing matters. And the sooner you realize that, the sooner you can do all the filthy little things you've always wanted to do. So what do you say, Mr. Channing? Are you ready to truly set yourself free?"

The Russian moved closer, flipping the seat backward and letting his knees bump against Officer Channing's. "Am I making you feel uncomfortable?"

"Leave my family out of this."

He chuckled. "It's too late for that. And let me tell you. Your wife didn't complain. Not with me anyway."

Officer Channing's heart raced. "I don't believe a word you're saying."

"You don't have to. Just know this. I've only just begun. You're going to keep playing your part, and you're not going to stop playing your part until we say so. Now here's the thing. I'm going to get what I want. *We're* going to get what *we* want. The only question is when. And it will be easier on you if it's sooner rather than later. You'll get your little payoff. We'll make the evidence disappear."

"You planted that evidence!"

"That's never stopped you. It never changed what the jury believed. And it won't make a difference with you either. So let me ask you again, Mr. Channing. Are you going to do what we ask you this time with a little more enthusiasm, like you believe it? Or do you want me to pay a few more visits to that little wife of yours, not that she minds it?"

Officer Channing balled his fist and gritted his teeth but said nothing.

"Good. I'm glad we understand each other. But I don't mind coming back here. A guy can get lonely in my line of work," he said, placing a zipped gym bag on the ground, which clinked as it touched the floor.

Officer Channing let him walk out of the shed, then spit in his direction when the door closed. He opened the bag and sorted through its contents.

A short while later, Officer Channing returned to the bedroom. Warm steam filled the air, with the sound of running water coming from the closed bathroom door. He stepped toward the dresser and picked up his wedding photo from its top surface, touching his wife's face, then placing the photo face down with a stoic expression. He stepped back, picked up the gym bag, and left.

CHAPTER 13

The Array, August 2, 2025, day 1, timeline 1
1:16 p.m.

ONLY A FEW minutes remained for Quinn to make the adjustment. Several shrieks echoed through the hallway. Quinn shivered, then shrugged it off, moving into position within the barrier section to reroute the array's electrical power to the external rod.

Ambient static powered low-energy-consumption illumination, so the panels alone presented electrocution risk. Only a portion of the power was artificially generated, which meant he couldn't completely shut down all electrical systems, but he didn't need to. If he could deplete those not generated by the magnetic field, he could prevent a short within the section. A few sparks flew from nearby panels.

Once Quinn pried open the panel, he entered the system passcode and began rerouting internal pathways. The array wasn't designed to intentionally deplete the modest amount of electrical energy, so he had to find command codes that forced blockages within the system's logic. This also required accessing several nearby shutoff valves manually, and he had to access each separately.

"What's the situation?" Jeremy asked over the walkie, which Quinn had switched permanently on so he didn't have to fiddle with it while working. "I hope you're making faster progress than I am. I think I'll scrape under the wire with section nine. But I don't think I can make it to the other section in time."

Jeremy didn't respond. Quinn turned three shutoff valves and two rerouting switches in quick succession. He tested the electrical pathways, but they didn't show any depletion. Then he realized he missed one of the energy regulator backups. A few moments later, he entered the reroute codes, squeezed through the barrier section, and jumped on the portable jumper.

"Section nine's been neutralized. I'm heading to meet up with Gary. What's your status?" Quinn asked.

"I think we're almost there, but we're still running a few seconds behind. I don't think we're going to make it," Jeremy said.

"But we've got another problem. The messenger is working against us. I don't know how he's accessed the emergency shutoff, but he has, and he's slowing it down. We may have to think about splitting up the array," Sam added.

A high-frequency pitch squealed over the walkie. "I think Gary's trying to call into a different frequency. I'll need to switch bands to pick up, so I'm going dark for a bit," Jeremy said.

In section seven, Gary continued coding away, attempting to reverse everything the messenger was doing.

"Jeremy, I can't reroute electrical from section seven. The

system's been compromised. I can already see the antimatter injectors activated from within the inner rings. I've jerry rigged some code to delay the antimatter transport, but it won't stop it. We might be able to stop the section overloads, but that's the least of our problems now. We're going to have to decouple all three sections. Tell Quinn to begin decoupling from section nine. You and Sam will navigate section eight from the main control room. The messenger's rerouted communications, blocking access to local station chiefs, so it's up to us."

"What about the walkies?" Jeremy asked.

"I haven't been able to contact anyone else beyond these three segments. The messenger might have found a way to block the signals."

Gary sat back in his chair mod and slid on his visor. "I hope I don't regret this," he said.

Static echoed through Quinn's walkie. "Quinn, you there?" He didn't answer, instead tapping on the external door to open the hatch into the control room.

"You gotta go back. Now! It's too late. The systems are going to overload. The injectors are running the antimatter through the inner rings now. We need to decouple all three sections of the ship. Get back to section nine and reconnect the power. You'll need it for the decoupling."

Quinn's face warmed, turning red. He nodded then returned back without saying anything. A few minutes later, a jolt shook the array, tossing Quinn off the jumper. He steadied himself and hopped back on. Fifteen seconds later, the hallways emitted a low-pitched hum which signaled local magnetic relays powering down. The jumper was useless without them.

Quinn bolted into the direction of the barrier section.

If he didn't get there in time, he'd be stuck on section eight with the command center and unable to separate the other two segments. If that happened, the two larger sections would have too much inertia going in one direction.

Illumination flashes pulsed through the hallway. Quinn kept running, pushing his body to its upper limit. His legs burned, and he felt like he needed to hurl. The hum returned with a higher frequency. It rapidly cycled up, signaling reinitialization and a coming antimatter injection. Only this time, nodes weren't connected to siphon off the juice. It would hit the outer rings and cause a catastrophic system failure, something that shouldn't be possible.

Quinn exhaled, reflecting on what he could've done, if anything, to prevent that sort of thing. There were only so many safeguards he could have implemented without making the project unfeasible. It became a trade-off between saving the world in 2021 or worrying about design flaws that would only be a problem if super hackers from the future managed to infiltrate the system.

A few seconds later, Quinn collapsed in exhaustion on the right side of section nine. He slammed the manual control, initiating decoupling from tier one. Gary would have to separate tier three.

"I've activated decoupling. What's Gary's status?" Quinn asked over the walkie.

"We haven't heard back from him yet. It sounds like he's having some interference from the messenger. I think—"

The walkie cut off before Jeremy could finish. The hum cycled higher. The illumination pulsed faster. For a brief moment, artificial gravity blinked, creating pockets of weak spots, not enough to make Quinn float, but enough to know the antimatter injectors had reached the array's middle rings.

Quinn opened the panel and read the current array configuration. The antimatter would hit the outer rings in seventeen seconds. Even then, he'd still have some time to reactivate the magnetic coils before the antimatter interacted with normal matter from beyond the outer rings, but not long.

Quinn tapped the walkie. "Jeremy, can you hear me?" No response. Quinn entered additional commands within the access panel, attempting to reactivate magnetic coils, which Gary had shut off but now needed to reactivate.

Several indicators on the panel displayed the level of antimatter flow and flashed red, indicating several system overloads and critical parameters. Over the hum, a low echo beeped from a nearby access port.

"Quinn. Are you there?" Sam said.

"I can hear you. What's our status?"

"I've been able to partially restore array comms, and I've notified station chiefs, but they've been locked out. The good news is that Gary was able to decouple tier three from section ten. You'll have to run tier-one navigation from a backup manual relay station two levels up. Gary discovered that the messenger was trying to get access to navigation relays by attempting to force him to network array segments. He failed, thankfully."

"Finally, some good news. How much time do we have?" Quinn asked before stopping once he realized the comms failed again.

Quinn double-checked panel readouts, but the display blinked then flashed off. Sparks shot out from the panel. Quinn hopped onto the ladder leading to section two. The array's comms crackled.

"Quinny," the voice said, drawing out the *y* as he spoke. "Oh, Quinny boy. It's not going to work," the voice said.

He ignored the messenger and continued toward level two. Halfway up the stairs, a large container tumbled toward Quinn. "Who's there?" Quinn said.

"It's just me," the voice said.

"And who's that exactly? An alien? Time traveler from the future? Terrorist?" Quinn asked as he continued climbing. Only a few more rungs separated him from the next level. Before he could climb higher, a nearby panel shot out sparks in his direction and seared the fabric surrounding his wrists. Earlier, Quinn anticipated the messenger might try to use the array's circuitry to attack him, just as it did to Sam.

"Quinny boy. You're not going to win. No, no, no. Not going to win," the voice said.

"What's your deal? What are you trying to do?"

"Isn't it obvious?"

"No. Not at all. That's why I asked."

"You'll find out soon enough. On second thought, maybe you won't. Can't find out if you're not alive to see it."

"Then why don't you tell me what's going on," Quinn said as he reached the final rung.

Quinn catapulted toward the panel he needed to secure the decoupling. A high-pitched wail echoed loudly across the array, signaling the antimatter filling into the outer rings. Quinn had less than a minute to re-engage the magnetic coil. In either case, he would have to go through the decoupling and could reconnect the array once the emergency was contained. If not, he'd have to navigate tier one of the array away from Earth and direct the antimatter into targeted bursts through a series of release ports.

"It's over. Might as well give up now," the voice said.

"Why are you afraid to tell me what's really going on? Worried I'll find a way to fix things?" Quinn asked.

At this point, Quinn was convinced the voice was from the future. Alien, human, AI, he didn't really care. He almost asked if the messenger was afraid he'd undo what was being done, but he wasn't about to give the game away on the outside chance the voice was just a good old-fashioned terrorist.

"I'm not afraid. I just don't feel the need to help you out, Quinny boy."

"Why do you keep calling me that? Do you know me?" he said.

Quinn kept entering the decoupling instructions while activating a preprogrammed set of navigation instructions that would activate within thirty seconds of decoupling if he didn't cancel the sequence.

"Don't you like being called that? You are like a little boy. But I think you already know who I am, or who we are."

Quinn had a clue but wasn't certain. He'd suspected the voice was connected to Vladimir, trying to instigate chaos to throw Quinn off track. But if that were the case, he wondered why they'd waited until now to show up. Why not just destroy the array in 2021?

"Ha ha. There we go," Quinn said. The navigation code kicked in and began initializing.

"It's too late," the voice said.

"Yeah, we'll see about that."

For a brief second, the magnetic coils reinitialized. "There we go. There we go," Quinn repeated. A few seconds later, a low-pitched wail signaled deactivation.

"Told you it wasn't going to be that easy."

Only ten seconds remained before the auto navigation set tier one on a path to deep space. Nine. Eight. Seven. Six. Five. Four. Three. Two. One.

CHAPTER 14

S<small>EPTEMBER</small> 2, 1984, <small>DAY</small> 111, F<small>RANK'S BODY</small>
8:42 <small>A.M.</small>

Quinn woke to Kathy sitting next to him, stroking his forehead.

"How are you feeling?"

He debated for a second whether to tell her the truth. He sat up. "I've got something I need to explain. It's nothing bad, well, I guess it depends on how you look at it. Strange might be more accurate. But it's something I need a bit more time to explain, and after coffee."

A short while later, they finished off breakfast, and Quinn downed his second cup loaded with more cream and sugar than he'd ever used in his lifetime. As much as he hated Starbucks, he missed it more than ever.

"This is going to sound nuts. I mean frothing-at-the-mouth, looney bin nuts. But I'll be able to prove it if you stay with me."

Her face turned ghost white. "You're scaring me now. What is this?"

Over the next half hour, he explained everything from

his first loop in 2021 to the array and back again. He provided as much detail as he could remember in the short time and then dove into the subject of the recent loops in Frank's body. After he finished, she stood silent for nearly a minute before saying anything.

"I don't get it."

"What don't you get?"

"I just don't get it. This is pretty disgusting. I mean, my son? This thing is way over the line, whatever this is. It's sick and perverted, and I don't want anything to do with it."

"Just follow me to the window. I want to show you something."

"No. I don't think so. I'm not playing whatever game this is."

"Wait, just give me twenty seconds. I promise I—"

She cut him off. "I gave you half an hour. I'm not giving you any more. You've been acting strange since Saturday, and I don't know what's gotten into you, but I need some space from whatever this is."

"Just twenty more seconds. That's it. That's all I need."

"Maybe that's all you need, but I'm going to need a helluva lot more."

September 2, 1984, day 112, Frank's body
8:42 a.m.

Quinn woke to Kathy sitting next to him, stroking his forehead.

"How are you feeling?"

"I'll let you know after coffee. But I've got something I want to show you," he said.

This time, he gave into small talk, waiting for the moment he knew what was going to happen.

"Let's go to the window," he said. "See that bird over there in the street?"

"Yeah?"

"A scraggly gray cat is going to jump on it in a few seconds. The cat will almost catch it. A few of its feathers will fly off, but so will the bird a second later."

She wrinkled her forehead and opened her mouth as if about to say something then stopped herself. A moment later, the scene played out just as he'd predicted. She stared at him then glanced back out the window, repeating the motion a few times before finally speaking.

"How did you do that?"

"I'm not done. Look down the street toward the end half a block down. You see that brown Pinto on the left side? In about ten seconds, the alarm is going to go off. A few seconds after that, some half-naked woman is going to start running after a man who's running toward the car. When she catches up with him, she's going to beat him over the head with a tacky orange purse. He's going to drive off, and she's going to jump on the hood to try to stop him."

The expression on her face said she wasn't sure if she believed him but wanted to see if it played out. Ten seconds later, just as he'd predicted, the alarm went off. A man ran toward the car. A lady wearing nothing but her underwear ran after him and beat him over the head. She hopped on the hood of the car when he drove off.

Kathy said nothing, opening her mouth then closing it before she spoke.

"Do you need more?"

"What are you telling me? What's going on?" she said. "I'm feeling light-headed. I need to sit down."

She didn't make it to the chair. Instead, she collapsed on the floor. When she came to, Quinn held a cold washcloth over her forehead. "Here. Drink some water."

He held the cup to her mouth as she drank, then set it down. He gave her a few minutes to gain her composure, then walked her to the sofa and waited until she was safely leaning back.

"That was the easy part. What I'm about to tell you next you'll need to brace yourself for."

He repeated the explanation. This time, he tidied up his delivery and inserted a few more qualifiers. He spoke in a more empathetic tone, added a few more positive notes, and leaned into the possibility of what might be to come. Forty minutes later, he finished. Once he stopped, her breath became shallow. Seconds later, she fainted again.

That time, she slept. Quinn rested by the window as he waited for her to wake and inspected each interaction on the street level as if analyzing the probability of each. A few hours later, she mumbled something unintelligible before becoming more alert.

"Was I dreaming?"

Quinn smiled. "You might have been, but everything I showed you out the window and told you about did happen."

"Tell me again, just so I know for sure."

"I'll give you the short version. I'm your son from the future and woke up in Dad's body yesterday. I started looping time after a supernova nearly destroyed the planet, but I managed to find a way to stop it. And for whatever reason, four years after I did, I got shot back through time, only this time with a twist," he said.

"This can't be true. I mean, I still must be dreaming."

"Pinch yourself."

"What?"

"Pinch yourself. See if you can feel it."

She complied, and then she winced. "There has to be another explanation."

"Do you need to see more? I've got all day, heck, all eternity—" he paused "—I think, to keep doing this. I mean, there might be this convergence of the multiverse thing," he said, stopping himself. "Maybe that's it. Convergence."

"I'm not following what you're saying."

"You don't need to. But I just realized I might have overlooked something. It might help me get back."

Over the next hour, Quinn explained more in detail about the coming events and periodically reminded her of his ability as they observed predictions through the window.

Then he asked Kathy, "Can you stay here? I need to talk with Dr. Green. Today hasn't happened yet, so I need to fill him in on the events and get the ball rolling."

She nodded, and a few minutes later, he was off.

During the current loop, Quinn ate lunch with Dr. Green near Saad's apartment. They both penciled through physics proofs in between turns of scoping out the surroundings.

"So do you think it might have something to do with this convergence you mentioned in the future, a shrinking of lanes in the multiverse within our nearby cluster?" Quinn asked.

"Maybe, but I've been pondering a possible scenario we might consider trying."

Quinn felt as if Dr. Green had been with him with each loop. He was so quick on the uptake that once he got past the initial disbelief, he was all in. The bits of information Quinn gave him regarding the math were all he needed to connect the next couple of dots. But Quinn knew at some point he was going to wake up the next day.

Quinn continued to reflect on the math, which had him starting in a different direction. In between cars, a figure hurried across the street in the direction of the apartment.

"Hey, I've seen that guy before. Not here, but about fifteen years in the future. At least, I think that's him," Quinn said.

Quinn quickly moved behind a large, nearby container to avoid being spotted. "Get down," Quinn whispered.

"We look a bit out of place here, don't you think?"

Quinn glanced around. From his squatting position on the busy sidewalk next to dozens of packed shops, it was definitely just a matter of time before someone drove by and blew their meager cover.

"Hey, you. What are you doing?" the young boy no older than four asked Quinn.

"Shhh. I'm playing hide-and-seek."

The boy smiled and shook his head then also spotted Dr. Green. "He's over here," the boy shouted, then began firing a large water pistol in Quinn's direction.

Across the street, the man who Quinn spotted turned in their direction looking directly at Quinn's location, which he could only assume was compromised.

September 2, 1984, day 113, Frank's body
1:27 p.m.

Quinn arrived with Dr. Green outside Hell's Kitchen. He'd already begun the process of planning another day forward, but before he did that, he'd need to uncover what Vladimir, the man he recognized, was up to.

They'd carefully chosen the perfect outfits to blend in.

With each loop, Quinn picked up additional '80s fashion tips from the clerks selling him his disguises, which they assumed were outfits to wear to low-key functions where he wanted to come off as unassuming.

After an efficient detour into an unpretentious clothing store, Quinn and Dr. Green sat at a small table in a video shop nearby. Quinn watched all the familiar players step into their expected pattern, from the little boy with the water pistol to Mark Channing and his partner.

He'd set his watch a minute before the much younger Vladimir was expected to arrive. Dr. Green would continue working on the equations and would swing into action to plant the bugs in the apartment and car once the two men arrived at Saad's apartment.

Kathy was out in the city deciding on how best to earn and spend some cash. Which Quinn would make happen once he got back just in time for the show. He was looking forward to it this time, since he wouldn't have to worry about his handsy mom trying to cop a feel.

"There he is," Quinn said, moving into position. Up close, Vladimir almost came off as handsome, with not quite a square jaw, but most women would find him attractive. Dr. Green stayed back, waiting for his cue to walk across the street. Quinn continued forward and situated himself behind a short young couple roughly twenty feet behind Vladimir.

Shortly before reaching Saad's apartment, Vladimir stopped. Quinn stood still as the scene played out in front of him. Two goons entered the stairwell. When they did, Vladimir moved closer but out of view from Dr. Green.

Dr. Green moved closer to the car, and Vladimir reacted with surprise, pulling out a notepad and jotting something down, but didn't leave his current spot. A moment later,

Vladimir signaled to Officer Channing, who was already casing the corner.

Quinn began putting some of the pieces together. They must all be working together—Vladimir, Saad, the goons, Officer Channing. And then he considered the implications for the future. The terrorist, or whomever they were working with, must have been laying the groundwork for decades. It was a complex web that Quinn wondered if he could ever completely unravel.

Quinn let Officer Channing and the other cops question then arrest Dr. Green. Saad and the other two goons soon left the apartment, and Vladimir held his position, watching.

Quinn realized he'd only noticed Vladimir based on his own shifting location near the apartment. He wondered if those pulling the strings were as meticulous with every location they operated from. While he considered the possibility, Vladimir stayed in position and didn't move for hours.

Quinn eyed the time, which was getting close to when he'd need to leave for the show with Kathy. He used every available second, noticing no visible movement in Vladimir until it was time to leave.

Forty minutes later, Quinn met Kathy near Broadway and Forty-Second Street. She wore a subdued outfit, for the '80s at least, but still classy. "So how did everything go?" she asked.

"I think I might be onto something with some of the key players. Back in 2021, I saw this Russian, Vladimir, working on the truck bomb that contained the exotic matter. I spotted him again, this time as what I think was a lookout or something for Saad and two other goons near Saad's apartment. And I think Mark Channing is covering for them somehow. Maybe acting as a lookout as well," Quinn said.

Kathy forced a smile on her uncertain face. "That's progress, I guess. At least you can come back and do it again tomorrow," she said before pausing. "Have we seen this show before?"

Quinn smiled. "Nope. Not this one. We've seen a few, but I was saving this one for the first time I told you. You can tell me if you want to see it again for the next do-over. What about you? Any ideas?"

"The lottery. I want to win the lottery."

"That's tomorrow. I'll have to move forward one day if we do that."

"Oh."

"It's not a problem. I mean, I guess it could be, but we can still do it. I just need to take care of a few things first. Maybe discover what Vladimir is up to. But honestly, I don't know if I will. It's a needle in a haystack. What they're planning could be weeks, months, or years in the future. And it's not like they're just going to come out and tell me. And if I find a way back, it won't even matter. All this has happened before, mostly, anyway."

Her brows furrowed. "Wait. So you're saying you can't stop any part of what they're doing?"

"No, I don't think I can. It's all going to play out on its own. At least, I think that's how it works. It's just like a maze. And we each have to find our own path in the maze. Every time we think we make a change, we're really just deciding which path in the maze we're going to take, but the maze itself doesn't change."

"That sounds a bit sad."

"It's more complicated than that, but I think it's kind of poetic. It's as if free will and predestination had a baby. I just haven't figured out the mind switch thing yet, if I even know what I'm talking about on the other stuff. I think for that you'll have to put the maze in a computer simulation within a simulation; then it might be closer to what's actually happening. It's all in the math somewhere, but I don't know if I'll ever find it," Quinn said. His face spoke uncertainty, defeat even.

"Hey, don't talk like that. You're my son, and I know you're like centuries old or something, but don't give up now. Whatever universe or path or whatever you're on, you'll find a way. I'm just glad you're not your father having an affair. 'Cause then you would really have a problem," she said.

Quinn smiled. "Let's enjoy this show," he said. She put her arm around him, and this time he didn't feel weird about it. It was a different kind of affection. And for the first time in a while, he wasn't just going through the motions. He had genuine hope.

Quinn thought he knew time was fickle. Every time Quinn felt that way, some twist of fate, or the multiverse, always had a way of shuffling the deck of life.

They maneuvered into their seats, and for the next ninety minutes, they engrossed themselves in each costume, leg kick, flourish, and proclamation by the actors. Quinn lost himself in the red carpet and drapery, and for the next hour and a half, he let go of his burden and immersed himself in the show.

"That was something else," Kathy said on the way out the door. "How much are we paying for all this, by the way? I'm assuming it came out of our savings."

"The great thing about looping time is that money isn't usually too much of a concern. But I always keep an eye on days that I have let ride, so I can conserve or invest. But we're going to be lottery winners, so you won't need to worry about that too much."

Kathy stopped for a few seconds. "I was thinking about that. Do you think it might draw too much attention to us? If this group and these people are as bad as you say they are, maybe it's not such a good idea."

"I think you might be right. It'd be a quick payday, but we could do it more slowly in the stock market."

"What happens if you're able to find a way back? Will I forget all this? Will it all be undone?"

"I don't think so. You'll continue moving forward, and I'll just have hopped into a different path."

"Does that mean I'll have your father back?"

Quinn thought a moment before speaking. "That's our working theory. I still haven't figured all that out yet. The math and physics are a bit complicated, but I think that's what will happen."

They slipped into the flow of the crowd through the exit then turned right toward Central Park. He hailed a taxi. "I want you to meet Dr. Green," Quinn said.

Just as they were about to enter the cab, a loud midfrequency bang popped nearby. Kathy's eyes widened, and she turned toward Quinn.

He looked down, noticing a red splotch getting bigger near her stomach and growing by the second. Two more shots rang out in quick succession. She collapsed to the ground. Quinn quickly turned in both directions, hoping to catch a glimpse of who fired the shot, but there was nothing.

He held his dying mother, realizing every timeline would play out once he left. In this one, his father would be alone once he returned, and Quinn would never be born.

CHAPTER 15

THE ARRAY, AUGUST 21, 2025, DAY 1, TIMELINE 1
1:20 P.M.

"HA HA. I told you it was too late. Now my work is done," the voice said.

Quinn inspected the navigation holo, which showed tier one was moving quickly out toward deep space. With the decoupling, internal spinning halted. Only exotic matter provided partial gravity and inertial dampening.

Sensors flickered different colors, sirens wailed, and all objects not tied down shifted to the left corner of the room where Quinn worked. Moments later, comms flickered back on.

Quinn attempted to hail Gary and Jeremy in the other array tiers. He used alternate communications, which still failed. He repeated the process with the station chiefs in various sections of tier two and three. Nothing.

"This is Quinn Black. Can anyone hear me?" Quinn said over tier-one comms.

"This is chief Juan Morales of section eleven. I hear you loud and clear. Readouts from my terminal show a complete blackout from the rest of the array, but I'm able to access all channels within tier one except for comms beyond section twelve," he said in a watered-down South African accent.

"It's good to hear someone else's voice."

"Likewise, Mr. Black."

"I'm going to need your help restoring the magnetic coils to the outer ring portion. But to do that, we'll need to reinitialize the micro vents to siphon off some residual antimatter," Quinn said.

"I've got seven crew members between sections eleven and thirteen. We'll need to climb into the outer shaft and manually reconnect the port couplings to the magnetic coils. The problem is that emergency systems are blocking reconnection. So we'll have to find a way to override them manually, which won't be easy to do," Juan said.

Quinn reflected on array schematics, which he'd designed. He remembered from initial planning he'd put in several alternating barriers within each ring, all of which could be magnetized.

"Give me a couple of minutes. We might not have to do that if I can send a signal by rerouting some of the backup connectors. I just don't know if our little visitor is still with us. Go ahead and set up your team, but I don't want to send them in there just yet. In the meantime, see if you can contact the remaining tier chiefs and begin a coordinated response to Earth to let them know what's going on. My readouts are limited. I think it might have something to do with the interference we've been having from the 'messenger,' or so we're calling it," Quinn said.

Quinn punched the seven-digit code to access the backup computer panels. He navigated the surface-level code to see if he could maneuver some of the navigation systems into the emergency throttles, which might provide what they needed.

A siren sounded, indicating a malfunction in one of the release valves. Several pipes provided emergency relief pressure from various flow interchanges that could mechanically activate certain transfer functions of the array, which included everything from electron flow and magnetic coils to static pressure and atmospheric conversion.

"Standing by to execute manual override," Juan said over the comms.

"Almost there. Just another minute," Quinn replied.

Immediately following the reply, tier one shook.

"We're breaking up. Partial internal dampening is failing," Juan shouted.

That could mean only one thing. Exotic matter had been extracted from critical segments within the array, and that couldn't be done electronically. If the messenger was from the future, Quinn surmised he had to be working with someone on the array.

Quinn's hands fluttered over the readout holo and switched between each segment on tier one. A third of the section was experiencing catastrophic integrity failure, which threatened coil breach.

"Juan, we need to get a team as far as we can starboard. We'll need to split tier one into two smaller segments if we're going to stop this breach," Quinn said.

"My team can't make it in time. The trams are down, and even then the distance is too great."

"Have you been able to signal the other segment chiefs?"

"All comms are down. Walkies are nonfunctional. I have access to some system logs, but none are current. But I can see readouts," Juan added.

"I have an idea. What if we intentionally create a malfunction in the relay panels? We can use the emergency sequence to alert them to the problem. We could send a basic message using an alternating light pattern. They'll have to be looking at the readouts to pick it up, but I think it's a good bet at least a couple will. All we need is someone in one of the starboard segments to pick up on it and decouple the bridge connectors. Once they pick up on the signal, we'll be able to communicate by using messages through system logs," Quinn said.

"On it," Juan replied.

Quinn continued to navigate backup transfer functions, but reactivating the magnetic coils was unlikely, given the acceleration and gravity loss. Exotic matter executed several critical systems and reduced mass and energy requirements for rapid transfer and navigation, as well as structural integrity.

With the inability to reinitialize magnetic coils, or rather the potential harm in doing so, Quinn's sole task shifted to navigation until he could think of another way to reduce the array's inertia without hull failure.

The other problem was that everyone in tier one was about to die, at least if they weren't able to split the section into two separate segments, and fast. Antimatter injections would come in direct contact with normal matter and annihilate everyone in seconds.

Quinn's heart skipped a beat. He toggled back and forth between the progress being made on the additional separation and the current navigational status. He felt like he was stuck in a loop, refreshing the screen over and over again, hoping at some point it would show him what he wanted to see.

Several minutes flew by, and Quinn hadn't heard a peep

from the messenger. He was beginning to think either the distance from the other tiers cut off communications or the messenger was actually on one of the other tiers.

Quinn tapped the control panel, rolling his fingers while he racked his brain for something he could do, either to find a way to speed up the separation or to rescue the crew.

With catastrophic failure, it was unlikely the crew would be able to get at a safe enough distance to save themselves. And then there was the problem of Earth. If they did manage to save themselves using the shuttles, they would likely sacrifice Earth in the process.

Each crew member's function was primarily related to the transport and regulation of antimatter and storage nodes. They hadn't been trained for all the microscopic possibilities if they found themselves hurtling through space.

"How are things coming with those relay panels?" Quinn asked Juan over the comms.

"Just activated the last one. If they notice the message, we should be getting a response soon."

Quinn read through systems logs. Most were dry reading, discussions of prior and upcoming transfers, the occasional relay panel replacement, and antimatter inventory reports. The most interesting logs came from the cleanup crew.

They handled the jobs the rest of the personnel detested, but this made them an eclectic group of characters. Most people might call them misfits, anarchists even, but the majority were just free spirits who didn't give a rip about what anyone else thought. And paradoxically, they were also the most kind-hearted group of the bunch, usually working on the job to help pay for family back home.

Cleanup crew logs generally lacked the usual communication protocols. Six months after the supernova, Quinn instituted the Array Academy to streamline array functions and personnel. But the cleanup crew were some of the most valuable members on the array precisely because they did the jobs that most people, including academy recruits and graduates, didn't want to do.

Several cleanup crew logs mentioned an external warehouse that had been modified to convert 3D printer recyclers into magnetic coil regulators and navigation components. In between colorful words and work summaries, Quinn picked up on a common thread with many of the logs. Over the past year, they built up a patchwork of underground systems that often handled basic operations better than the original design specs of the official components and system regulators.

The patchwork underground was by no means complete, and it was primarily for disposal and repair, but Quinn considered if it might be possible to access the underground systems to assist them.

As he continued to read, a new system log alert popped up.

> THIS IS RAYCON GRILL, SYSTEM CHIEF 487 ON THE STARBOARD SECTION. I'VE PICKED UP ON YOUR MESSAGE. I'VE ALREADY SENT ALL PERSONNEL IN MY SEGMENT TO ACTIVATE EMERGENCY SEPARATION PROTOCOLS. IF ANY OTHER SECTION CHIEFS BETWEEN 389 AND 501 READ THIS MESSAGE, I COULD USE YOUR HELP IN THE REALIGNMENT COUPLINGS.

"Juan, are you there? The section 487 station chief picked up on our signal and has started working on the separation. But I was reading through the station logs and noticed this underground array network run by cleanup. I was thinking we might be able to use some of its functionality to speed up the process."

"How's that?"

"For one, they seem to have scraped up enough exotic matter from recycling funnel ports to activate certain system modes. If we can access one of their warehouse stations, we might be able to patch together enough exotic matter to secure hull integrity to reactivate the magnetic coils. We'll still need to go through with the separation, but it may buy us enough time."

Maybe realigning the magnetic coils wasn't off the table after all, that is if they were able to split tier one into two separate sections.

"That's brilliant," Juan said, in his distinctive South African accent. "I've got one of those warehouses right next door and a couple indispensable crew members who can get started on this section."

"Get on it. And I'll place another message in the logs informing the chiefs to do the same thing at each of the warehouses. All we need is a few strategic placements, and I'll relay the coordinates," Quinn said.

Quinn went back to work finding an alternate way to rejoin the magnetic coils. If they were able to pull off the placement of residual exotic matter, he could realign the magnetic coils and stop the antimatter breach.

He entered a few more commands to reactivate transfer and initiate magnetic coil relocation. They wouldn't have much time since the antimatter was already pushing up against the outer rings, but they'd need to wait until structural integrity was reinforced before initializing. Otherwise, they'd rip themselves apart, which would create a breach of its own.

Several minutes passed. Quinn managed to reconfigure all the settings and simply needed to execute the command to begin realignment. He glanced at the station logs and noticed several more messages. They popped off faster than he could read them. Apparently, station chiefs from all over tier one noticed the signal. Separation was nearly complete.

Tier one shook. Objects near Quinn shifted again. At first, only a few items moved. Soon, larger objects repositioned themselves.

One of the station logs caught Quinn's eye. Section chiefs identified several critical junctions in each segment and forced exotic matter into a specific set of 3D-printed pipe connectors laced with dark matter. They attached couplings and positioned them into the corner of each critical section in certain rooms.

Quinn tapped on the comms. "Panel readouts indicate we're no longer in jeopardy of a breach, at least for now. But we're going to keep adding those pipe mods in critical systems. I'm reactivating magnetic coils now. But I'll have to access the override relay at the lower level."

Quinn executed the command, but the magnetic coils wouldn't reinitialize until the hard connection sent a signal from the override relay panel.

As Quinn headed toward the ladder, he got his first good look around since he'd arrived at his current position. He'd expected to see a complete mess, but only a few items in each room weren't secured in some way, so there wasn't much evidence of the partial gravity failure except for the occasional misplaced chair or crate.

A few rungs down the ladder, another jolt dislodged his grip. He slipped, flailing most of the way down before he latched onto one of the rungs near the bottom. "Ahhh," he cried out, pulling his torso toward the ladder.

His head throbbed. His ribs sent sharp pains through his left abdomen. Once he secured himself, he continued his descent until his feet touched the floor. He rambled toward the panel, then steadied himself. "I'm at the lower level now, Juan. Notify the station chiefs," he said.

Quinn pulled the handle hard, struggling with his weakened side, then reinforced it with his other hand until it was more than halfway up. Next, he shifted his weight, pushing until it clamped shut.

A low-pitched hum wailed through tier one. Lights flashed in the hall. Colored indicators flickered from the panel relay indicating tier-wide comms should be working. Quinn tapped the comms panel and entered the station section. "Mr. Raycon Grill, this is Quinn. I've reinitialized the magnetic coils. I'm going to need to command the starboard section of tier one. Follow emergency protocols."

With magnetic coils realigned, Quinn attempted to restore localized electrical flow and the magnetized floor to power the trams and allow for normal system functioning. While comms were operational on tier one, they still lacked communications with the other array tiers, which Quinn assumed was interference from the messenger.

Quinn breathed deeply and exhaled, then activated the final protocol for full reinitialization of all tier systems. Then a long blue-and-white electrical bolt radiated from the panel and branched out, striking Quinn, who collapsed onto the floor.

CHAPTER 16

Sᴇᴘᴛᴇᴍʙᴇʀ 3, 1984, ᴅᴀʏ 1, Fʀᴀɴᴋ's ʙᴏᴅʏ
7:00 ᴀ.ᴍ.

THE ALARM SOUNDED. Quinn sprung up and eyed the room. He was alone in the tiny apartment. For whatever reason, he hadn't been able to loop the day. He dialed Dr. Green. "Something went wrong. I wasn't able to go back."

Dr. Green held his response. "I . . . I . . . think I might know the reason."

Quinn's skin warmed, and his stomach sank.

"I don't think you'll be able to go back before today. At least not while you're in your father's body. Kathy's death may have severed the connection between you and your younger self."

"Then why didn't I just go back to the future?"

"This is still a bit of guesswork. I don't have an answer for you. I'm still not even sure if that's the reason you weren't able to loop. But from what you told me, the default is just to move forward one day if something's amiss."

"This is going to be a problem. Aside from living in my father's body, I've screwed everything up in this timeline," he said. Then he remembered what he already knew. He was just surfing lanes in the multiverse. He didn't really change anything. But that didn't make it any less difficult for him to be stuck in a lane that sucked.

Quinn wondered if that was what it felt like to all the people he interacted with who couldn't hop lanes like he could. It almost felt like payback, vengeance. He wondered if he was permanently stuck this time, and how much different things would be. No family other than his grandparents and a few aunts and uncles.

Quinn suggested meeting at Dr. Green's place, but Dr. Green didn't want to disturb his wife and wasn't ready to expose his collection of baseball memorabilia, which he'd curated from a young age, which he said was displayed on his wall.

"Then can you come over to my place?" Quinn asked.

Dr. Green agreed. Shortly after 8:00 a.m., he arrived at the apartment with supplies, diagrams, a small chalkboard, and a few pieces of electronic equipment he'd scraped together from his lab.

"I think we may have a bigger problem than what to do about your looping," Dr. Green said, dropping the supplies onto the table. "That Russian you were tracking," he said as he fumbled for something on the table, "I'm almost positive I saw him on my way here."

"I wonder if he's the person who killed my mom," Quinn said.

Dr. Green stood for a moment staring blankly at Quinn. "I'm supposed to say something, right? Like, I'm sorry for your loss. Or something like that."

Quinn's stomach twisted in knots. He knew the five stages of grief, and he had a perfect reason to stay in denial for the foreseeable future. "I'm not accepting it. Not if I can change it."

"But you can't change it. You know you can't. At least not in this timeline, not for your father, and not for you."

Quinn's fingers tightened around the chair, his short fingernails making marks in the wood. Dr. Green was right: Quinn couldn't do anything for this universe. And although he might be able to navigate to another one, he'd agreed with himself a long time ago to appreciate every life and mourn every death. But that time hadn't arrived. He was entitled to his denial, at least for another day.

"We can't stay here long. Not with Vladimir scoping us out."

Dr. Green interrupted. "Did you finish with the police last night?"

"That's it. You're a genius."

Dr. Green looked confused.

"I told them I couldn't talk last night, was not in the right frame of mind. I could call them over now. That would give us some cover, keep Vladimir from doing anything too provocative while we think about our next move."

Dr. Green listened but continued fumbling around until he found a clunky, square electronic readout that reminded Quinn of the massive cell phones found in that era but with a small screen with a green-and-white digital display.

"What does that measure? Tachyons?" Quinn said with a half smile.

"Not exactly, but I have been experimenting with neutrino fluxes. You mentioned before that I mentioned in the future that a conflagration of multiverses could compress to a single cluster of possibilities. I've been doing the math, and I was thinking, changes in the neutrino pattern might hint at a change in the supernova you said will arrive in a few decades."

Quinn let Dr. Green blather on about his theory and several different ideas about what might have changed. While he did, Quinn dialed the officer's number who he had spoken with the prior night. A cup of coffee later, someone knocked on the door.

Quinn peered through the peephole then let the officers in, Mark Channing and the cop who looked like a stern Robert Patrick from *Terminator 2* among them.

The officers pushed their way through the door as Quinn stepped back. "So let me get this straight, Mr. Black."

Quinn already felt his blood pressure rising.

"You had just left a Broadway show, and for no apparent reason other than the fact that you were there, someone just shot in your direction?" Officer Channing said.

"Not sure if they were actually shooting in my direction or if we just happened to be blocking what they wanted to shoot. And I didn't see where they were coming from or who fired the shots, but, yeah. That about sums it up," Quinn said, pausing while looking straight at Officer Channing.

For a fleeting second, Quinn thought he caught an uncertain glare from Officer Channing. "Do you go to a lot of Broadway shows, Mr. Black?" he asked.

"What difference does *that* make? My—" he paused "—wife is dead."

The other officers scribbled in their notepads during the conversation. "And who are you?" Officer Channing asked, turning toward Dr. Green, his face emotionless.

"I'm a professor at Columbia. What difference does it make?"

The other officer's eyes widened. "I'm just trying to get a sense of what's happening. That's all."

"Is it, though? The man's wife just died, and here you are berating us for no good reason," Dr. Green said.

"Listen, you called us, remember? You could have waited until tomorrow. Unless that is, you have something to hide."

"That doesn't mean you can harass the man. He's just lost his—" he hesitated "—wife, for Christ's sake. Just ask what you came here for and leave. We've got things to do. You know, like visiting her body in the morgue, making funeral arrangements, calling every single known relative he hasn't already just to make sure they know she's dead. Unless that is, you'd like to do that for us," he said.

"That's quite all right, Mr.—?"

"Never mind that. Just get what you came here for and leave," Dr. Green replied.

Quinn considered how they were going to get out of there while Dr. Green did a fine job of delaying them.

"Was there anything else you might need from us down at the station?" he asked.

"Can't think of anything off the top of my head. I can take your statement right here. Why do you ask? Is there something you haven't told us? Usually people are looking for a way not to come down to the station."

"I just don't want to have to come down there later in case there's something you forgot to ask us."

Dr. Green glanced out the window.

"Is there someone looking for you? Maybe there's something you're not letting on? And if I'm being honest, it feels like there's something you're hiding from us."

Quinn wanted to throw his words back in his face.

"You'd be jumpy too if you'd just been shot at and someone killed your wife."

A car backfired as it drove past them on the street outside. Quinn jumped. His left hand trembled, and he steadied it with his right.

"I'll be honest with you, Officer. I'm scared. I'm tired, and I'm scared. I didn't get any sleep last night. I still can't believe this is happening. And despite the fact Dr. Green is with me, I just don't feel like being in this apartment right now. Would it be too much to ask for you to let us ride with you to the station and you ask us the rest of your questions there?"

Officer Channing squinted and turned to the other officers. "Not sure what you really want, Mr. Black. You guys are all over the place. Your friend telling us to leave and you wanting to hang out with us, but if that's what you want, I can take you to the station."

Dr. Green began gathering his things.

"But not your friend, Professor Columbia, there," Officer Channing said.

"Why can't he come too?"

"Was he there when it happened?"

"No."

"Then there's your answer. We're busy at the station, doing things that busy cops do, and we don't want or need people there who'll just get in the way," he said.

Quinn considered the situation and how things might play out. If Vladimir was casing the apartment, he'd be coming after them, but drawing his attention was the lesser of the two evils.

Dr. Green locked eyes on Quinn, nodding in approval. "Fine. Go ahead without me. I'll hold the fort down here, you know, in case someone needs help with the funeral arrangements or some such."

On the way out, Quinn faced straight ahead but eyed both directions of the street and scanned ahead. He spotted a brown-and-white late-'70s-model Buick station wagon and someone who could have fit Vladimir's description from a distance.

At the station, Quinn inspected the setup, which was almost exactly as he remembered it from the time they picked him up after escaping the clinic. It was tough to read cops from their mannerisms. Most were trained to appear emotionless. Experts call it emotion-regulation training. Quinn knew from experience that it doesn't always work. But he wasn't getting anything from these cops.

He sat at Officer Channing's desk rattling off semi-rehearsed responses in a distracted daze.

Channing gave Quinn a look of condolence. "That's it, Mr. Black. If there's anything else, we'll let you know. And I'm sorry for your loss."

"Thank you," he replied. Officer Channing's response made Quinn question his thoughts about him. In the future, he was a prick, just like his son before things changed. But he wasn't as hard as he expected, and he expressed what Quinn felt might be genuine empathy. His colleagues, however, appeared robotic and cold.

Once out the door, Quinn hailed a taxi. It was the same Pakistani driver who'd picked him up before. The coincidence made Quinn consider whether it might be serendipity or something more sinister.

"Where to?" the driver said in a thick Pakistani accent.

The cab was unassuming at first glance, but on closer inspection, Quinn noticed two small photos near the meter, both of a young boy and attractive woman whom Quinn assumed were the driver's family.

Quinn gave the address then said, "But I need you to slow down a few blocks before we get there."

The driver furrowed his brow. "You got it."

During the drive over, Quinn took in the sights of Manhattan. Oddly, 1984 was growing on him, Michael Jackson jackets and all. He let the concerns wash over him, still embracing the first stage of grief, denial.

Closer to the address, the driver slowed. "We're almost there. What do you need me to do?"

Quinn eyed the Buick half a block up. "Here is fine," Quinn said. "Just let the meter run. I need to think."

They sat there for several minutes until the hunk of brown-and-white metal began to move. "Follow that car, but stay far enough behind that he doesn't see us."

The driver followed Vladimir several blocks then turned onto a main street into heavy traffic. They continued for twenty minutes until the Buick turned into a parking structure in Midtown. "Here's fine," Quinn said, handing the driver the fare plus too much for a tip before he ran out ahead of the next car.

Quinn positioned himself out of view of the Buick and waited for Vladimir, who sat in his car for ten minutes before finally moving toward the direction of the main library.

Quinn held his distance until Vladimir disappeared, then quickly ran across the street and entered the library.

The younger Vladimir approached a middle-aged, plump woman with a name tag, but Quinn couldn't make out anything they said. She directed him toward another area of the library. Once they began to move, Quinn followed.

Later that evening, Officer Mark Channing sat at the dining table with his young wife, Meredith, and two-year-old son. At that age, she was angelic, not too thin, and a commanding presence. "Something's bothering you, I can tell," she said.

She held their toddler, Scott, on her left leg, feeding him with a fork from a small porcelain plate.

Mark exhaled. "Just a lot on my mind. Things haven't been going the way I'd hoped."

She stared at him. "What kind of things?"

"Has anyone been here?" he said, pausing. "Anyone come to see me?"

She sat little Scott down on a small chair nearby then returned to the table. "You know I don't like it when you bring people here. I don't feel safe."

"I don't always have a choice. Police business, you know."

"No, I don't know. Can't you take care of that business at the station? And what kind of business?"

"You know I can't talk to you about work. I'm not allowed to, and I wouldn't want to put you in danger."

"You've already put me in danger."

"What do you mean, exactly? Did something happen, something you're not telling me?" Mark asked.

Meredith shook her head. "You know I would never do anything to hurt you, right?"

"What's that supposed to mean?"

"It means I put up with this even though I don't like it. And I handle myself. Don't you get it? These men, and I don't believe they're all cops, maybe, what do you call them, your snitches?"

"Informants."

"Whatever. They shouldn't be coming here. You're smart enough to know that."

"I told you, I don't have a—"

"Choice? That's a lie, and you know it. You always have a choice." He could tell she was about to add something then stopped herself. "What happens if one of these informants hurts us or puts us in some kind of danger? This has to stop. Our son needs this to stop. You still love me, don't you? I know you love your son at least. Make this stop."

He sighed again, pausing. "I have a few things I need to take care of first. You don't understand. I'll take care of it. I will. I just need some time."

"Do better. And don't take too long."

He lowered his head a few inches in acknowledgment. Then something rustled from the outside.

CHAPTER 17

Sептемвеr 4, 1984, day 1, Frank's body
7:30 a.m.

"WHY DIDN'T YOU loop time yesterday?" Dr. Green asked.

"How do you know I didn't? Maybe I looped it an infinite number of times and this is just the branch where I didn't," Quinn said.

"You do have a point. So is that what you did, or were you unable to loop time again? Or maybe you looped it a few times and found what you needed?"

Quinn's face said he needed more rest. His eyes appeared tired, vulnerable. "I just couldn't stop thinking about Mom, the way those goons gunned her down. Or at least I'm assuming they're the same Russians that are working with Vladimir. I tried to go back again. Figured I owed her that much, even though I know it doesn't help her in the other timelines."

Quinn could tell Dr. Green was trying to think of what to say.

"I didn't notice any other Russians last night after you left. I'm pretty sure the one drove off when you went down to the station, but I did make some progress with one of the time travel theories," he said.

"At least one plan worked," Quinn said.

They spent the better part of the morning discussing what Dr. Green found and then scrutinized the area before slipping off to the library.

They scoped out the exterior for several minutes once they arrived, then around ten found the section of the library where Quinn saw Vladimir the previous day.

The special reference section contained ephemera, relics, and rare manuscripts. It contained two additional rows of tables, one on either side of where they stood, and some of the sections required ladders to reach the upper shelves, which held the larger and older books. Quinn assumed the practice kept people from overhandling them, but he was surprised they were so out in the open and not stored behind glass or in a back room.

Most of the books were tan or dark brown, hand sewn with vellum binding. Many had ridges, and a few had faint water markings on the outside cover. A musty odor, which reminded Quinn of a damp cellar, emanated from the books and hung in the air close to the shelves.

Dr. Green beamed from the moment they arrived, and Quinn found him inspecting the title *Don Quixote*. Dr. Green quickly scanned the level then moved on to the next one. He mouthed a few words, which Quinn couldn't make out, then counted silently with his fingers as if picking up on a pattern of some kind.

Quinn scoured the shelves, unsure of what he was looking for or what Vladimir was doing the previous night. A different librarian was there from the night prior, this one an unassuming guy in his early thirties. "These are very interesting books, but I don't see a lot of people in this area. What do people usually check out from this section?"

The man smiled. "Usually they're looking for a first edition of something, but we don't really carry those. These are mostly hand-scribed books from Europe, the Middle East, and North Africa. Recently, though, we've had a lot of interest in small sections on antiquity, necromancy, and fortune-telling," he said, directing Quinn to the section which Dr. Green was already inspecting.

"I see your friend's already found it. The one he's holding has been very popular the last few months. It contains images of ancient symbols which people have claimed to have spotted at seminal events throughout history."

"Do you mind if I take this?" Dr. Green asked.

"You'll have to keep that here, unfortunately. And for security purposes, you'll need a slip just to read it at the table. Most of these are one of a kind," he said, directing Dr. Green to the local desk, where he filled out his information.

They sat at the table, closely inspecting the book's imagery, which was all hand drawn. Quinn was expecting something alien, maybe from the pyramids, but all he saw were hooded figures, a few symbols which seemed to indicate messages of some kind.

A few minutes later, the librarian said, "We do have one in Middle English, which you might be able to understand."

"Yeah, I'd like to see that one," Dr. Green said.

The librarian slid the ladder into position and climbed to the very top shelf, carefully handling a large leather-bound book. It was thick, dark brown, and over two feet long with heavy ridges along the spine. "Be careful with the pages. They're a bit brittle," he said, handing them a special set of gloves to use for turning the pages.

Quinn noticed raised bumps that reminded him of braille. He traced the front through the glove's fabric. When he opened the leather-bound cover, he turned the first page, which was thicker than he'd expected, like it was improperly cut or a few pages glued together.

They sat there for hours. The first two they spent engrossed in the book, inspecting each page until they reached the end. In the back, they found a few thinner pages, like they were attached later. Those pages contained a list of historical events going back to the Egyptians. Large clusters of dates existed during certain times, the Pax Romana, the fall of Rome. But then there were periods with large gaps.

"Look at this," Dr. Green said, pointing to the last section of entries.

"These dates are in the future," Quinn said.

"But this one is recent, the same day I arrived."

"And look at this one," Dr. Green added. "This is tomorrow. And this picture almost looks like, like—" he said, pausing.

"The space shuttle," Quinn finished.

Dr. Green's face lit up and eyes widened. "I don't think you're the only one. I think there have been others like you. And maybe, just maybe, they've been stuck."

"You think this is their way of trying to leave the world a message, change events in their favor?" Quinn asked.

"Or maybe communicate with someone else. And if they can, maybe you can too," Dr. Green said.

"But how? And with who?"

"We just need to keep looking."

"I need to go back to yesterday, get a closer look at what Vladimir was looking at."

September 3, 1984, day 2, Frank's body
7:00 a.m.

The alarm sounded. Quinn sprung up and eyed the room. He read the calendar and turned on the news to confirm he'd been able to repeat the day. After he was satisfied, he called Dr. Green and filled him in.

This time, he left the apartment early and met up with Dr. Green for breakfast near the library before it opened. They both put on ridiculous disguises that made them look older and more assuming, but their goal was to blend in at a distance so they could discover exactly which book Vladimir was reading once he arrived, assuming he'd arrive after they'd changed events.

Hour after hour, they took turns on lookout. Whoever had off spent the time working on the equations. It felt like a futile attempt to cobble together a theory that Quinn didn't have much faith would work. But they didn't want to stop on the off chance they made a discovery Quinn knew breakthroughs happened from time to time with enough persistence.

At 1:37 p.m., much earlier than the prior timeline, Vladimir arrived. Quinn was on watch and tapped Dr. Green, who perked up.

They both held books out in front of them and peered above the top, waiting for Vladimir to make his move. He spoke with the same woman, but for a few minutes longer than last time. A few minutes later, she used the ladder and climbed to the second shelf from the top near the left side of the shelf.

From their distance, Quinn noticed the small book was

a light tan color with dark markings he couldn't make out. Vladimir opened the book near the middle and turned a few pages until he found a page near the center of the book.

Vladimir studied the pages for a few minutes, writing something on a notepad.

Quinn scribbled a note to Dr. Green, who nodded in agreement once he read it.

Once Vladimir returned the book to the librarian, they both strolled at a medium-brisk pace toward him. Dr. Green took the route closer, and Quinn stood farther away. Just as Dr. Green was nearly upon him, he snatched the notepad from Vladimir and tossed it toward Quinn, who caught it and ran.

Vladimir bolted toward the door in the direction of Quinn. As they ran, Quinn read the notes and wrinkled his face. Quinn ran into several people on his way out, then tripped just as he stepped onto the sidewalk. His head hit the pavement, and he blacked out.

September 3, 1984, day 3, Frank's body
7:00 a.m.

The alarm sounded. Quinn sprung up and eyed the room. After he was satisfied he had arrived on the prior day, he called Dr. Green and filled him in.

They met for breakfast at a different location. This time, he splurged for a high-end establishment on Fifth Avenue near the library, where they ate and discussed Quinn's finding from the prior loop until the library opened.

"I'd like a book from the second shelf from the top," Quinn said to the librarian.

"What's the title?"

"Don't know the title, but I can point it out to you."

She appeared confused but followed Quinn to the shelf. "It's the light-colored one, third from the left, second shelf from the top, the one with the dark markings on the spine."

She hesitated. Quinn thought she was about to speak, but then she retrieved the book from the shelf. She took her time on the computer, appearing agitated, then after a few minutes, handed it over with the special gloves.

Dr. Green and Quinn thumbed through the center of the book, comparing the writing to the vague notes Quinn remembered from his short glimpse at Vladimir's notepad, which hadn't been much help since most of it was in Russian. But he did see a few odd shapes, which he drew from memory the best he could.

"Look at this," Dr. Green said. "This word here, that's Latin for *energy*. And this symbol, it resembles a theoretical form of exotic matter found in high-energy states. I can't be sure, but I think these are instructions of some kind."

He flipped the page and pointed to a series of symbols below the last line of text. "And these here, I think they're blueprints to a device."

On the next page, a series of diagrams next to celestial events covered the page, including an image of what suspiciously resembled the space shuttle next to what appeared to be some type of man-made satellite.

"Is there a shuttle in space now?" Quinn asked.

"There is, as a matter of fact. And it just happens to be launching a communications satellite."

Quinn considered the revelation. "You think NASA's working with the Russians?"

"I think someone who worked on the satellite might

be working with the Russians, maybe even the people who designed it."

"Do you know anyone who reads Latin fluently?"

"I know a colleague who just might help," Dr. Green said.

September 3, 1984, day 4, Frank's body
7:00 a.m.

The alarm sounded. Quinn sprung up, eyed the room, and called Dr. Green.

They met for breakfast at another swanky breakfast joint. This time, one more expensive and a block down from the library.

Following a detailed discussion on what they'd found the prior day, Quinn said, "We need to rob the library."

CHAPTER 18

THE ARRAY, AUGUST 21, 2025, DAY 1, TIMELINE 1
1:33 P.M.

"I'VE GOT SEPARATION!" Gary shouted over the comms to the command station. He waited a second, scanning the navigation controls. "But I don't have enough distance. My nav system still lacks power. Is there any way you can provide a boost from command?"

"That's a negative. And we've got our own navigation issue to worry about. Quinn was able to set auto nav and already has some distance, but we're having the same problem you are. When we depleted the electrical and shut the magnetic coils, it separated access from our reserves. I can get them back online, but it will take time." Jeremy paused. A few seconds later he finished his sentence over comms. "Too much time. We need a plan B."

Gary thought he heard something from the outside door. "Give me a minute. I'll get right back to you," he said. Gary heeled up and activated the exit. He rolled out and viewed both directions of the hallway near his modified port office and thought he briefly caught a glance of someone on the left side, then returned inside.

"Are you still getting interference from the messenger?" Gary asked.

"All kinds of interference. Can't tell if it's from our little visitor or what, but much of it doesn't make any sense. The frequency bands are bleeding all over our holos and interrupting our readouts. But I think we might have a solution to restore partial power."

Gary's section shook. "What was that?"

Just then, one of the local section chiefs, Titus, barged in with three of the cleanup crew. "We've got a problem. A piece of debris just slammed into one of the ports. We're venting atmosphere, and we don't have anything to plug it up without getting sucked out along with it," Titus said.

Gary pulled up the section on his monitor. It covered an eight-by-thirteen-foot span in the most vulnerable area. "What about the warehouse? Don't we have reams of alloy sheets lined with reinforced nanocarbon?"

"That's the first thing I thought of, but it's missing."

"How is that possible?"

"It's not. Not unless somebody stole it right from under our noses."

Now the discrepancies in the security footage were starting to make sense. And it had to have been a coordinated effort. Without weeks of analysis, there was no way for him to trust anyone. Everyone was suspect, including Chief Titus.

"What about the portable nodes? There's tons of reinforced material we need with each distribution."

"The problem is the closest one is too far away to do us any good," Titus said.

"What about the 3D printers?"

"Offline. It's the only option I can think of, but it's suffering from the same backup system energy failure as the rest of tier three once the section's energy was depleted."

"I know the printers can run on battery power, and the last time I checked, we had a ton of those."

"Our nearest supply was stored in the same place as the alloy sheets."

Gary's knees buckled from another shock, as did the three men around him. "What if we rip a couple walls from one of the sections. We should have a portable laser close by in one of the maintenance bays."

An odd odor filled the room, something Gary couldn't quite place, perhaps a mix of burning plastic combined with a hint of something he thought might be more toxic.

"I've already sent some crew members to look, but the maintenance bays have all been wiped clean."

Gary's eyes widened. "This is deliberate. Every single option we have, someone's thought of and gone out of their way to make sure we can't do it."

"Sure looks that way," Titus said.

The next moment, bright flashing sirens blared. "Systems failure imminent. Critical breach," the message repeated on a nonstop loop. Then Gary remembered his modified room contained a few sections he'd sealed off.

"I think I might have something," he shouted over the message. He hurried to the far inner side of the floor near his room's outer wall. He lifted a floor panel and pulled out a small cabinet. He opened one of its drawers and retrieved a microthin sealant.

The sealant was made from a genetically modified spider's web mixed with superstrong nanofibers. It could spray a bubble that conformed to just about any shape needed.

Usually, it was used for smaller tasks as a mega glue, but it could also create superthin bubbles that could seal off the breach until they found a more permanent solution.

"I'll take care of this," Gary said. He threw on a portable helmet and pushed the back-left bottom roller skate heel to the ground activating turbo mode. Then he rolled off into the direction of the breach.

Half a section down, the air was already thin and pulling him toward the direction of the hole. Three larger pieces of the wall ripped off in front of him, one larger in size than the prior section, which briefly covered a portion of the breach before it was sucked out along with it.

The force of the vortex pulled him close, but he managed to grab hold of a reinforced bar. The sealant container flew from his pocket, but he snatched the handle and flicked on the switch before it slipped from reach. Once the sealant exited the container, a spidery transparent bubble shot out in the direction of the breach.

The sealant worked by instantly drying once it came in contact with a hard surface but provided give for a couple of seconds if it didn't smack a surface. The sealant split the breach in two but sealed off the center portion. Gary's inertia carried him forward, but he kicked his motorized wheels into reverse, grabbed hold of the sealant container's handle, which had caught on the newly created center barrier, and sprayed each section until the breach had been completely sealed.

He turned his motors off, wheeled back, and inspected the web of a mess he'd just created. It was a dirty eyesore but would more than hold. He felt confident he could keep it as a permanent feature while maintaining structural integrity, but knew it looked too scary not to reinforce with alloy sheets as soon as they located some.

Gary returned to his office port and pulled up comms. "Any progress on energy systems?" he asked Jeremy.

"None, and we haven't been able to contact Quinn either. We're still experiencing system-wide disruptions, but we have been able to access one of the relay panels and begin siphoning off one of the reserve tanks."

"I think I got that little bugger where it counts, and he's exacting his revenge. Whoever this messenger is, maybe he thinks he's in a game or something, because he wants to destroy everything. That's the only consistent thing I've seen from what he's tried to do so far," Gary said.

"What do you mean by that?" Sam asked.

"The program attempted to get me to network the critical components of the array. And the only reason I can think he would want that is to vent all the antimatter freely and destroy everything in this solar system."

The array shook, interrupting Gary.

"I threw up some hidden firewalls embedded in the system environment, hoping he wouldn't detect it before it was too late. Now he's throwing a little temper tantrum. But we've got a bigger problem," Gary said.

"You think he's working with someone," Sam added.

"Exactly. My guess is they're still here somewhere."

"You think they're on a suicide mission?" Jeremy asked.

"Either that or they've been duped. But either way, our options are limited. The firewalls I erected will make it tough to access the residual energy funnels. I think abandoning the rest of the array may be our only choice. Quinn's already taken tier one at a distance, but I haven't been able to reach him over comms since he activated navigation."

The array shook. Gary lost his balance then activated his wheel motors. This time, the rocking continued for several seconds, like a major earthquake rattling everything attached to the ground.

"I've stopped the antimatter purge, but our visitor keeps reinitializing. And he's somehow managed to circumvent the shutoff systems each time we attempt to reactivate them," Sam said.

"He can't do that from a distance. It has to be someone here. If we can find them, maybe we can stop it the next time it happens and shut down the system for good. It's either that or we have to find a way to use some of the portables to launch the station into deep space and escape on some of the half-built ships in the docks," Jeremy said.

"I'll do what I can to assist. But my systems are jammed," Gary said, steadying himself as another tremor rocked the area where he stood.

CHAPTER 19

S‍eptember 3, 1984, day 37, Frank's body
8:03 a.m.

"YOU THINK IT'LL work?" Quinn asked. He'd spent the better part of the prior loop hatching a plan after a couple failed attempts at more modest thefts.

Dr. Green opened his mouth as if he were about to answer, then stopped himself before he finally replied, "Do you ever give up? Just take the year off and do whatever in the world you can *because* you can?"

"Within reason, but, yeah. In the future it's even easier to withdraw from everything. It's too easy. That's the problem. And then after a while, you find yourself sitting there, doing something stupid or watching something stupid or even achieving something that would be important if you were moving forward in linear time, but in the loop, it feels meaningless. Life starts to lose its purpose, and you feel alone, empty, like everything is pointless."

"What do you do then?"

Quinn smiled. "Live my life. Go forward. The danger, the chance, the limits of life and time add more value to each moment. And then, of course, you're not alone," he said before pausing.

"I think the thing that keeps me going when I have to keep looping is that I know what I'm doing is helping others. Or at least trying to."

"But is that really true? Aren't you just surfing the multiverse?"

Quinn thought about it before answering. "Yes and no. I'm not the only one who can surf the multiverse. Everyone else can too. They just do it differently. They can believe their choices have consequences, that if they want to improve they can. And a funny thing happens. Once they start to believe, their actions change. They change. So I do it for them, for those I can influence in each world who will see their actions matter."

"Yes, I think your plan will work," Dr. Green replied.

Quinn had considered the scenarios and thought their best chance at moving forward was bringing the book back to Columbia so Dr. Green's colleague could read through the highlighted passages. It would still take time to get through, but not nearly as long if they tried to decipher it all themselves.

Quinn chuckled. "All right then," he said. He allowed the absurdity of their appearance to sink in for the first time. They carted off their gear and headed out.

The plan to sneak in was ostentatious and dangerous. He just hoped no one would get killed in the process. And it also broke many of the seven rules. Quinn struggled with that in the beginning, but the more he considered it, the more he realized that the current timeline would likely end without stopping the supernova. Not to mention, his mother was dead, he wouldn't be born, and he needed to make a change regardless. His biggest concern was not killing anyone else in the process.

A short while later, they set up camp across the street from the library an hour before opening. Quinn observed the sights, sounds, and smells of the city. Before every big plan, that's what he always did, his way of showing gratitude for the present moment, whether in the past, the present, or an infinite loop.

The air was more polluted than in the future. Dozens of people stood in view on the sidewalk smoking and eating. Others strolled along sporting frizzy and crimped hair in tacky, bold, contrasting colors.

They positioned themselves on a large corner a block down on the other side. They used several large magazine stands as cover as they set up what to the outside observer looked like an industrial-sized sports bag used by PE teachers in school to hold dodgeballs and the like. On the bottom of the bag, they hid several smoke bombs and firecrackers.

"We can set them off there?" Dr. Green said, assembling the small team of bystanders they'd use as part of the distraction.

The plan was to create an unauthorized miniparade replete with a giant Stay-Puft Marshmallow Man they'd already stolen from a warehouse for the upcoming Macy's Christmas Day parade. They'd set it off in one direction nearby and draw the police as misdirection when they did a smash-and-grab on the library. It's funny how stealing float props was easier than breaking into the library, at least successfully. They'd pulled it off on the third try.

The smoke and fireworks would signal to the entourage of underage misfits they paid off with booze and cigarettes. It was for the greater good, of course. Quinn still felt a bit uneasy about the whole thing, but "desperate times" and all.

Dr. Green's math suggested that Quinn's window was shrinking, either from a narrowing cluster of possible outcomes or from the loss of residual exotic matter that hopefully still tethered him to his prior life.

They passed off the bag to the most vanilla character of the bunch. They handed him a timer reading fifteen minutes, and when it struck zero, the innocent-looking teenage boy would set off a slew of smoke, fire, and noise.

Quinn's synced timer dinged. A low-pitched bang rang off from the prior location, cuing them to pull out their window cutter and slice a hole in the side of the building.

"Almost there," Quinn said, spinning a circle large enough for both of them to slip through once he finished.

A few sirens blared in the distance but were soon drowned out by a never-ending stream of fireworks and then a marching band.

They entered the opening. Gray-and-white clouds drifted west behind them from the smoke bombs. More sirens wailed. They scampered toward the reference section with nothing but a backpack and their disguises, which consisted of fake beards and long, curly wigs.

In the first few loops, they didn't bother with a costume, figuring it would draw more attention to them if they did. Eventually, they tried a few and got farther with each iteration.

Fifty feet from the section, they strode past a dozen empty tables then spotted a security guard who'd just started his shift. He was short, bald, and a few decades past his prime, if he ever had one.

"Hey, you there. Stop where you're going."

They stepped up their pace and tossed a few smoke grenades toward the man, quickly obscuring the room. Twenty seconds later, they'd nabbed the book, stuffed it in the backpack, and made their way back.

They doubled back and were almost at the window when a second security guard stopped them in their tracks. Dr. Green grabbed another smoke bomb, but the small man behind them caught up and struck both of them on the back of the head. The room went black, and Quinn collapsed to the floor.

September 3, 1984, day 38, Frank's body
8:24 a.m.

They positioned themselves on a large corner a block down on the other side of the library. They kept the same set but hired a few more misfits to make a distraction on the Upper West Side and left a couple minutes earlier.

Quinn's synced timer dinged, but police sirens had already gone off a few blocks down. Now, a low-pitched bang rang off from the prior location.

Quinn rotated the window cutter blade faster, slicing a hole in the side of the building. A dozen more sirens blared in the distance but were soon drowned out by a never-ending stream of fireworks and then a marching band.

They entered the opening. Gray-and-white clouds drifted west behind them from the smoke bombs, this time more colorful along with a few streamers. More sirens wailed.

Quinn tossed two smoke grenades in the direction of the over-the-hill security guard and then threw one behind them near where the other guard had taken them by surprise. Dr. Green grabbed the book this time, and Quinn held a metal police rod they'd stolen in case they needed to trip one of the guards on the way out.

A dark mass approached from within the cloud of smoke and closed the distance as they approached the window. This time, they made it long enough for the Stay-Puft Marshmallow Man to make his appearance.

"Give that back," a voice yelled from behind Quinn, who ignored it, pushing forward.

Dr. Green slipped through the hole, but the second guard pulled on Quinn's leg. Quinn tripped. His head hit the metal lip of a nearby table on his way down. Darkness overcame him as he rolled again and struck the ground.

September 3, 1984, day 53, Frank's body
8:24 a.m.

Quinn and Dr. Green positioned themselves on the same large corner a block down on the other side from the library.

Quinn's synced timer dinged. They headed off toward the library, this time with two young misfits along for the ride. He couldn't help but feel guilty, wondering if he was contributing to their delinquency. But he'd come up with a solution that would hopefully put his mind at ease.

With the help of Dr. Green, Quinn created a list of letters that he'd mail out every day. Each would contain a major event in the coming decades, earthquakes and volcanic eruptions mostly. He'd also provided a list of all he knew about certain unsavory characters, drug kingpins, terrorists, and other information.

He fashioned the letters in the form of anonymous tips. He'd mail out some immediately, depending how close they were to the event, and he always mailed a few. He sent a couple to news outfits and people he trusted with every single one. He always sent several of each event to different people, just in case one or more didn't take the incidents seriously.

His hope was that the news outlets would come to trust the information as reliable, and at some point, they could begin evacuating locations when they needed before major occurrences and investigate those who needed investigating. But he also knew over time, the information related to the criminals and terrorists would become less reliable, so he kept that down to a minimum.

The most important of all, though, was the information regarding the supernova and the array the world would need to build to save the planet in Quinn's absence. He might be gone in some other universe when it occurred for them, but he at least wanted them to have a fighting chance.

With Dr. Green, they might just be able to pull it off, but Quinn would need to leave as detailed specs as possible, and it also would require a ton of money. So each loop, Quinn wrote a list of everything Dr. Green needed to become a billionaire in the future, which would be necessary if he were to have any success pulling off the rescue of the world in his absence.

Finally, Quinn created a list of deserving people, philanthropists, artists, inventors, all of whom had a rough go of it in the future. He told Dr. Green to mail each of the letters with information they could use to help nudge things in their favor.

The deliberate attempt to make the world better even after he'd hopped universes helped Quinn feel a little less bad about possibly turning the lot who were helping into even worse miscreants. But he had letters for them, too, which Dr. Green would mail in the event of Quinn's timely demise. And if Dr. Green died, then Quinn would just mail out the lot early.

A loud bang rang off in the distance, this time with twice

as many fireworks and in two groups, each on either side a block away from the library. The two teenage boys, both around fourteen, stayed back as Quinn cut into the glass. They wore clown wigs and large, baggy pants.

Once Quinn entered, the two teens followed. Dr. Green waited on the outside. Quinn tossed the smoke grenades like before and hurried to the reference section, where he leaped up onto the ladder and tilted the book over until it fell into his backpack.

"Stay there," the short, bald guard shouted. The smaller of the two boys ran toward him, then darted in the opposite direction.

Once Quinn made it to the window, the second guard was nearly on him. The taller boy blared a foghorn in the guard's direction. The guard jolted back momentarily then charged forward. By that time, all three slipped through the hole. The two boys tossed a couple more smoke grenades on the ground.

A few minutes later, all four removed their disguises in the smoke and blended into the crowds on the other side, walking at a normal pace. Quinn and Dr. Green faced forward and once they were one block away, flagged down the first taxi that approached.

The same Pakistani driver from before picked them up. Traffic slowed up ahead but continued to crawl forward. "Can you believe that? It's the Pillsbury Dough Boy," he said.

"I think it's the Stay-Puft Marshmallow Man from the new movie that's out, *Ghostbusters*," Quinn replied.

"Ah. I haven't seen it. Is it good?"

"The best," Quinn said as Mr. Stay-Puft grew in size as they approached, not as big as in the movies, but tall enough to draw a crowd.

Quinn opened the bag a crack and peeked in, smiling.

SEPTEMBER 3, 1984, DAY 53, FRANK'S BODY
1:23 P.M.

"Where did you get this?" asked Hattie, Dr. Green's Columbia associate.

Quinn cut Dr. Green off before he had a chance to reply. "My father collects antique books. He picked this one out from upstate from a rare book store."

"Which one? I think I've been to most of them in the area, but this is a find."

Quinn changed the subject. "No idea, but Dr. Green says you're an expert linguist, fluent in Latin. Do you speak Russian too?"

She smiled, which didn't match her otherwise strict appearance. "As a matter of fact."

Quinn pulled out a notepad and showed her the scribblings as best as he remembered them. It also helped that he'd spent a few feeble attempts at learning the language. He didn't remember any of it, but he at least recognized how to write the characters, mostly.

"Ah, that's interesting. It doesn't make complete sense, but I see a couple of words that might suggest something. Can you show me the part of the book you wanted me to look at?"

He wanted her to look at all of it, and that's what he planned to do, but they'd start with the center where they thought Vladimir had opened the book when they saw him inspecting it. Quinn opened the book to the page Dr. Green attempted to translate earlier.

Hattie squinted and almost touched the page, then

hovered over instead. "This is fascinating," she said, moving her finger across, line by line. She mumbled something, which Quinn assumed was in Latin.

"Can you read it?"

"I think so, but it's a bit cryptic. It mentions something about a visitor or visitors, not in this realm but another, not completely here or there."

"Like a message?" Dr. Green added.

"Maybe, but then it goes on in the next page to talk about a group, hidden in the shadows, or shadows falling down. I can't be too sure." She turned the page. "And then here, a way to bridge the divide, or grow the divide maybe. With something, a substance, a sphere. Power from the heavy wood."

Quinn frowned. "Does it say anything about time? Or maybe a way to find one's way back home?"

She turned the pages. "I don't see anything like that, but it does talk about a wanderer. Or wanderers."

"That's interesting," Dr. Green interrupted. "So you think it says there are more than one?"

"I believe so." She turned one more page. "No. Wait. I think it might be a chronology, an introduction to many wanderers. And some kind of discussion. A written history. I'd need to study this some more. You mind if I take this a few days?"

"We have to give it back soon. How much time do you have now?"

"A few hours at most, but that's not enough time to—"

Quinn interrupted, "That's perfect. Just do the best you can."

September 3, 1984, Day 127, Frank's body
1:23 p.m.

"Where did you get this?" Hattie asked.

Over the last two months' worth of loops, Quinn parsed as much from the document as he could. Each day, Hattie translated about fifteen pages, which got them through the book a few times, but each time got them closer to something resembling answers, the possibility of a way back.

Dr. Green did the honors of fabricating an elaborate story of an estate liquidation from a family needing to pay off their taxes from a dead relative.

Quinn filled her in on all the key parts, this time keeping her focused on a few relevant pages that they hadn't solved in the prior loop.

"You know a fair amount of Latin yourself. Where did you study?"

"Self-taught," Quinn replied. "But this is the part that's stumped me," he said. "What do you make of it?"

She read over the passage a few times. Then her eyes lit up.

"Oh, I see what it's saying now!" she said.

CHAPTER 20

Sептемвек 3, 1984, day 127, Frank's body
7:23 p.m.

THE RUSTLING OUTSIDE the house returned. Officer Channing knew what that meant, and he was sick of it. Sick of everything, the blackmail and turn of events.

He helped Meredith with dishes after dinner. She gave him a half smile. He hadn't helped in a while. He used to, but recently he hadn't been around all that much. And then he felt guilty. He worried she resented him for it, withdrawing, especially with their two-year-old, little Scott, in tow.

He wanted to believe her and not Vladimir, but his recent actions made him doubt it. Was he good enough for her anymore? Did she resent him for not being there? And he didn't understand what she was trying to say. He hated that, wished she would just come out and say instead of hinting at things, wanting him to read her mind. But he was getting better at reading the minds of criminals. He was starting to think they were all the same, out for themselves. Maybe everyone was out for themselves.

After finishing, he went around the back to the shed.

"There he is," Vladimir said.

He thought Vladimir wanted to say something about Meredith but held back.

"So have you come around to my way of thinking? Do you want to get out of this mess?"

"You mean the mess that *you* made?" Officer Channing asked.

"That you made," Vladimir quipped back. "Let's be clear about something here. I own you. I own that little wife of yours, that son of yours, but if you do what I say, I'll keep my distance. Promise. Cross my heart and hope to die," his thick accent bleeding through as he gestured with his fingers, drawing an *X* across his chest. "Now open the bag," he said.

Officer Channing complied, pulling out a dozen files he'd lifted illegally from the station. They included both officers and perps, every piece of dirt he knew about those who worked at the station and the informants who helped them.

Vladimir thumbed through the files until he found the one he was looking for, about Officer Channing's current captain, Aiden Burgos.

"Yes. This will do nicely," he said.

Underneath the files, the bag contained several spherical balls. Vladimir told him they were listening devices developed by the Russians. Channing didn't believe him, but didn't think they were anything more. He figured it was more of their telekinesis nonsense they were testing or something more ridiculous.

He'd poked and prodded the spheres, unable to find a way to open them. And he wasn't sure if Vladimir knew what they were either. He assumed Vlad was a pawn just like he was. Officer Channing wondered who pulled the strings,

Konstantin Chernenko perhaps, or maybe a crime syndicate that found its way into Manhattan.

Officer Channing pledged his life to the city, and when he did, all those years ago, he meant it. He was young, full of idealism and the desire to slow the raging crime that threatened to tear the city apart. And for a while, he thought he was making a difference. That all changed once Vladimir arrived.

The night before, Officer Channing thought he might have activated one of the spheres. Vladimir explained earlier what to do with them, which didn't make much sense if they were listening devices.

Vladimir retrieved a small reflective sphere from the bag and placed it on the table in front of them. The orb stood four inches in diameter and mirrored a perfect reflection of everything around them. He made a series of evenly spaced taps on the side, like some kind of Morse code.

The orb split in two, with the top half popping up a few inches higher. A small steam cloud burst from the center, quickly reversed in on itself, creating a suction, then reversed again. The steam changed colors from green to gray and dissipated into a thin mist that emanated from the orb.

"What is this? This doesn't look like any listening device I've ever seen. What aren't you telling me?"

"Don't worry about it."

"What do you mean, don't worry about it? I don't care what kind of crap you've got on me, what you've planted, or what you plan to do to me if I—"

Vladimir cut him off, "And don't forget your wife and little boy. What I will do to them. Don't just think about yourself. Do it for them."

"Do what for them, exactly? I'm not doing a damn thing

if you don't tell me. If that thing is some kind of bomb, I'm not going to be responsible for that. I'll take a fall if I have to."

"And what about them? Are you okay with your wife being implicated too?"

He thought for a moment, fighting back the surge of adrenaline and mix of fear, trying to make sense of it all.

Vladimir palmed Channing's face, like an older man comforting a younger boy even though Vladimir was the younger one. "It's going to be okay. It's not a bomb. I promise."

Officer Channing wasn't convinced but wasn't sure his doubt was enough to make him refuse, especially if it meant everyone he cared about would be hurt if he said no.

"Listen. It's what it's always about, power and money. That's all. People I work for need to hold their power, and that's what I'm here for. Sure a few people will get hurt, but not at your hands. I'll do that part myself. This here," he said, palming the orb, "this is something else entirely, a prototype. A very sophisticated prototype, but a prototype nonetheless."

"Are all these prototypes? How do they work? I've never seen anything like this before."

"Details, details. Don't let too much sweat drip from that little head of yours. They are listening devices, but that's not all they can do, of course. You're smart enough to see that. But these here, we will extract them later when no one's looking. Or should I say, you will extract them? They'll give us the information we need, and then we'll be on our way. You'll get your money."

Officer Channing almost replied that he didn't want his money but said nothing.

"And then I'll eliminate the evidence."

"The evidence *you* planted," he replied.

"Come on now. You know your hands aren't completely

clean. That's why I chose you. You made a decision a few years ago, and I'm sure at the time you probably hesitated, wondering if it would come back to haunt you. And now it has. So listen again. I'll take care of that little thing. And then you can go about your career not worrying about that little secret. And I'll leave you alone. Simply plant the devices where I told you, and then retrieve them in a couple of days. They'll be invisible while they are working, so you won't have to worry about a thing."

Vladimir was right. For all practical purposes, Officer Channing had decided to plant evidence, and from that moment on, things got murky. He had a hard time deciding what the right thing was, who the good guys were, and even whether he wanted to continue as a cop. He told himself it had to be done, but he never truly believed it.

September 3, 1984, day 127, Frank's body
1:24 p.m.

Hattie's strict appearance softened. "See this here?" she said, pointing to several intricate symbols between the hand-scribed Latin characters. "The circles or, more accurately, spheres described in the passages are claimed to both emit and receive information and energy. And if you turn back to the pages in the back, there is a chronology that shows their first appearance. But the message predates the spheres."

"So you believe it's saying the message came before the spheres?"

"That's what it would seem to indicate. In the first few chapters, if you can call them that, you can see that communication was done with what looks like some kind of primitive radio signal," she said, pointing at the scribed crooked glyphs. "They coincide with specific celestial events, supernovas. You can see the one here in 185 AD. Then a few pages later, you see what looks like a drawing of some kind," she said, putting the book down and pulling out her laptop.

"I've seen this before." Her hand shook. "Yes! See this image. It's *Springs and Things*, a series of inventions by Leonardo da Vinci. The schematics look almost exactly the same, but that would mean the manuscript must have been made after da Vinci, but it doesn't match the markings here," she said, flipping backward and forward as she scoured through the symbols.

"Look here. It's instructions, glyphs recorded during intermittent periods of communication. At least that's what the images suggest."

"Communication with who?" Quinn asked.

Hattie inspected the markings on the current page and pointed. "This word here, *humanus*. It means 'human.'"

"So they were communicating with other humans?" Quinn said.

"That's what the manuscript suggests."

"Does it say how they discovered how to set up the original radio signals or communication system?" he added.

Hattie's brow dropped. "If you look here at this page, this was the first example of the word *communicatio* here next to the glyph depicting a rock outcrop. I think it's saying, based on the context of what's written around it, that minerals relayed a message, which was magnified by a celestial event, perhaps turning the rock enclave into some kind of radio signal."

"Wow! Are you saying this book is telling us that humans from somewhere have been contacting other people on the planet using rocks?" Quinn said.

"It appears to. And that's where things get interesting," she said.

Over the next several minutes, she laid out the case for a vast communication network while flipping between pages and glyphs. Quinn and Dr. Green volunteered only so much information, choosing to withhold the most critical aspects of what they knew.

She further explained how humans from somewhere else gave instructions on how to construct the first sphere, a device which she said the book promised would usher in a new age of peace and prosperity, a promise that neither Quinn nor Dr. Green believed was truthful.

A short while later, they met back at Quinn's apartment. They laid out their assumptions on what was happening with Quinn's shifting in time and how it might be related to both the supernova and the array. The manuscript added more possibilities, and they began to think that the group Vladimir worked for could have the solution they needed.

"I think Vladimir is either part of the same group or influenced by them, whoever's on the other side of that communication network," Quinn said.

"And if they had the dark matter bomb in the future, it stands to reason that they must have some of that now. We just need to find it," Dr. Green said.

"It's not at your colleague's apartment. They must be storing it somewhere else."

"The first place I'd look is that cop friend of yours, Officer Channing."

"My friend's father, but, yeah, I think you're right. But if he is storing it, what are you suggesting? We blow it up? If we do that, won't it kill everyone?" Quinn asked.

"From what you've told me, the bomb wasn't ready for

a few more decades. Maybe the orbs are just gathering the energy or dark matter somehow. If that's the case, it may be what you need to get back, and if you die in the process . . . ," Dr. Green said, hesitating, "well, maybe it's what you need to retether your mind to your own body in the future."

"So kill myself?" Quinn said.

Dr. Green shuffled through a few baseball cards he'd stuffed in his pocket, a set of common cards he didn't care about so much but mainly used for calculated stats.

"Dr. Green? Are you listening?"

Dr. Green stared a few more seconds at the cards before looking up. "Yes, kill yourself. You've done it before, or rather others have done it for you. Now all we have to do is locate Channing's address and get there sometime after he leaves. We just need to scope out his place this morning and see when he leaves, so you can loop back and arrive after he's left for work."

"We still have no idea if it will work. And if it doesn't, well, I still have my mother's funeral to plan," Quinn said.

The weight he'd been carrying tugged on his emotions. His mouth quivered, but he thought about the reality: it wasn't his mother. It was never his timeline, not like before. Everything that had happened wasn't his timeline. It couldn't be. Or could it? He was in his father's body. And his father never mentioned anything about sharing Quinn's thoughts or having his mind displaced. So whatever this was, Quinn was a visitor. He wondered if there were others.

Once again, he pushed down the emotion, reflecting instead on the great mother Kathy was and the great mother she would be again once he successfully killed himself and traveled back to the future.

CHAPTER 21

THE ARRAY, AUGUST 21, 2025, DAY 1, TIMELINE 1
1:47 P.M.

"LOOKS LIKE YOU'RE not omnipotent after all," Gary said, wondering if the messenger was listening.

Gary tapped the comms. "All systems, I've restored internal station comms on tier three and partially restored backup functions. I need all of you to gather all supplies. Do an inventory of all critical components. I suspect sabotage, so I want everyone working in groups of three and all inventory and systems triple-checked. I've managed to regain control of most systems and downcycled antimatter injectors, but until we can get the magnetic coils reinitialized, we're still at risk."

Gary turned off the comms for a moment, collecting his thoughts and considering the next command. "I need all the cleanup crew to immediately begin working on repairs. We've lost external communication to tier one but still have a line with tier two. I'll keep you informed of the progress," he said, wishing he could log back into his game mod.

On the smaller tier two, which was essentially just a few array segments, Jeremy continued his attempt to contact the Long Island launch center or anyone from Earth. He'd settle for satellite communications, but the command section was completely shut off.

"Any progress with overrides?" he asked Sam.

"I've never seen anything like this. I mean, I haven't seen half the stuff I've seen in the last hour, so that's not exactly surprising. Whatever the interference is doing, it's like two competing lines of code battling each other, looping around then rewriting script as fast as it emerges. I seem to be able to find a few pockets where I can insert a few commands, but they're usually brief, and the other code rewrites them in a matter of seconds. But I think I'm seeing a pattern in the rewrites and might be able to gain a foothold, or at least slip something out from the program environment, but it would have to be small," Sam said.

"That's something at least. Keep trying. I'm feeling pretty useless. Haven't had much luck with anything," Jeremy added.

Sam said nothing. Jeremy was hoping for some reassurance to his own increasing self-doubt, but he knew they had their hands full. He wished he had Sam's confidence, or at least the confidence he used to have. Once they'd finished with the current crisis, he was going to take some time off to reassess, maybe go back to charity work or perhaps start a megacasino on the fledgling moon base. He wasn't sure which.

The entrance to the command center shook. Fingers slipped through the crack, prying the doors open.

Sam frowned. "Who is that?" they asked.

Jeremy wrinkled his brow. "Shouldn't be anyone," he

said, pulling a pistol from underneath the command station. Whoever they were, they remained quiet, trying to pry open the doors.

Sam kept working on the code. Jeremy stood up and lurched toward the door. "I'm ordering you to state your purpose. Why are you trying to breach the command doors?"

The hands finally separated the segments. He didn't recognize the person standing before them. They weren't wearing a uniform or clothing he recognized from array personnel. A figure face emerged, looking up toward Jeremy. He resembled a young boy, maybe thirteen or fourteen.

Jeremy didn't understand. There weren't any families living on the array. He'd had discussions about it, and it was inevitable at some point, but not yet. "Hey, kid. What do you think you're doing?"

"I think I'm going to kill you," the figure said in an altered mechanical voice. The boy tossed in a spherical ball, one that resembled the orb that Sam and Quinn had told him about, only smaller.

The ball was almost transparent, reflecting everything around it. It popped open. Jeremy lunged toward the orb, grabbed hold of it, then tossed it out through the door just before it went off.

The station shook. The emergency backup system walled up a thin shield of metallic walling around the immediate command section room. The material had spatial properties, designed as one of the safeguards in case of a system breach.

"Who are you? Why did you do that?" Jeremy asked.

Sam continued like nothing happened, still plugging away at the lines of code fluttering down the holo screen at their station.

The boy said nothing. A moment later, walling expanded

from within the command room. Externally, it took up no additional space, but the exotic matter lining the structure gave the command station additional square footage. And then the fun began.

Once the new walling activated, several additional command stations emerged from underneath the floor, unfolding from the edges where the old boundaries used to lie, then pushed outward toward the new internal perimeter.

"You don't deserve this. None of you do. You're not going to win. You're not going to stop us," the boy said.

Jeremy inspected him closer. His clothes contained no pockets, and Jeremy couldn't see any other weapons. "You sit right there and don't move," Jeremy said.

Sam continued quietly, their fingers working at lightning speed. They turned. "I think I've got something. I've managed to separate the fields of code. They're definitely separate and not coming from the same place."

The boy stepped closer.

"I said stay back," Jeremy said, pointing his gun at the boy.

"You can't beat us." The boy's eyes flashed.

"What are you?" Jeremy asked.

"We're like you. We are you. Only better," he replied.

"I don't think so. And I said stay right there."

The boy lunged toward Jeremy, grappling his arm, tugging at the gun. A battle ensued to secure the pistol. The boy flailed his arm around Jeremy faster than he should've been able to. Jeremy twisted, gripping the pistol barrel down and attempting to squirm his way out of the creepy hold the boy enacted around him.

Jeremy's face grimaced. "What are you? What are you doing?" he asked again. Jeremy leaned back then fell backward with the pistol behind his back. Jeremy thought he'd secured it, lying flat against the ground with the pistol pinned underneath the middle of his back, pinned by his arms.

The boy pulled back from his knees, sitting up on Jeremy. He smiled. "You won't win. You won't beat us."

The words sent a chill down Jeremy's spine, which the boy had pinned to the floor. A cold shiver trickled up Jeremy's skin, and the fine hairs covering them popped.

"I got it, little bastard," Sam said. "I've been able to quarantine half the code from the rest of the array's systems. We should be gaining systems any—"

Alerts interrupted them. Full lights flickered on then remained solid. A medium-pitched hum sounded, briefly increasing in pitch before stopping, signaling full power.

"I've restored full power. The other half of the code, it looks like it's . . . like it's helping us."

"Well, you mind helping me? I've got this creepy little demon thing on my chest. Help me get him off," Jeremy said.

Sam moved away from their station toward Jeremy and the boy. Once within arm's reach, Sam snatched the boy's arm and attempted to pull him off, but the boy's arms moved quickly, like they were sped up tenfold by pressing fast-forward.

The boy grinned. "You won't win. You won't win," he repeated. Jeremy finagled his right arm with the pistol from underneath his back and aimed the pistol toward the boy.

"Get off me now," he said, wondering if each second he hesitated would give the boy an opportunity to grab it away from him.

The boy's arms rapidly slapped Sam's in some kind of freaky pattern. Sam lunged backward and to the side away from the boy.

Jeremy aimed, then fired the pistol. A siren wailed from

within the room, an array protocol when a standard weapon was fired. Not that it mattered for structural integrity. The array's construction was bulletproof. It took something with much greater force to pierce containment. But it was the act itself, which signaled danger.

The boy's torso shifted back where the bullet struck it. Then he smiled. Jeremy shot the boy again, this time on the other arm. The boy nudged backward in the other direction but less, as if adapting to the new set of circumstances. His knees remained firmly planted on Jeremy's shins, still pinning him down.

"You won't beat us. You won't win," he repeated.

"You're a little brat, you know," Jeremy replied, pulling the trigger a few more times in quick succession. The boy barely budged. His eyes flashed again.

Sam yanked a section of electrical wiring still connected to the array's electrical circuitry and approached the boy from behind. The boy looked back as if he were about to lunge toward Sam. Jeremy fired his last bullet at the boy's half-turned back. The boy shot up off Jeremy. Once he was clear, Sam shoved the loose live metal wiring into the boy's face.

Flecks of bright white, blue, and yellow scattered from the point where the wires met the boy's face. The boy repeated himself, "You won't . . . You won't . . . You won't," in a feedback loop then collapsed onto the floor.

Sam approached the boy, still holding the wiring and clearly prepared to use it again if the boy sprung to life. Sam knelt down, getting closer to the boy, who'd finally stopped moving.

"I think he's dead," Sam said, lifting open one of the boy's eyelids. Jeremy approached and placed the extra bullet from his pocket into the chamber of the gun.

A stray red bead of light streaked down the boy's eyeball as Sam held the lid open.

"Oh crap," Sam said.

"What? You know what this thing is? Some kind of android from the future?"

"No, I don't think so," Sam said, kneeling closer. "Hold on a second. I need something to . . . Wait. Can you grab the medical kit?" Sam asked.

Jeremy strode toward the new souped-up med station, one of the terminals that unfolded after the exotic-matter-lined walling expanded the room. He rummaged around it until he located a shiny black box with a familiar red cross. He unlatched the clamps. "I got one," he said.

The open box revealed what Jeremy dubbed the first honest-to-goodness tricorder, though its functions were limited to scanning for known diseases and basic body functions. There was a needleless injector, small surgical instruments, several empty vials, small ports where fluids could be tested and analyzed, and a medical help recording device which was essentially a med bot to assist with problems stored in its limited programming.

Jeremy handed over the kit. By that time, Sam had pulled up a computer tablet and some thin translucent fiber cables connected to the station computer. Sam retrieved one of the vials and connected it to a small collection device then pressed it against the boy's arm.

Jeremy half expected nothing to happen, but then blood filtered into the small vial. Sam inserted the vial into the reader. A small holo screen lit up above the reader and displayed various readings. Jeremy activated the med bot.

A woman's face appeared on the holo screen. "I see you've already inserted a sample. How can I help you today?" the bot said.

"What does that sample mean? What can you tell us about the readings?" Jeremy asked.

The bot read a list of readings, all of which he didn't recognize except for cholesterol count and insulin levels.

"Are there any foreign objects in the blood? Something that shouldn't be there?" Sam asked, continuing to connect the fibers between the medical readout panel inside the box and the tablet. As they waited for the bot to respond, Sam pulled up schematics of some kind Jeremy couldn't see until Sam laid the tablet flat on the surface.

"Yes," the bot responded. "I'm detecting three thousand artificial metal objects."

"Can you tell us what the metal objects are?" Sam asked.

"Unfortunately not," the bot said, sounding almost human.

"What can you tell us about the objects?" Jeremy added.

"The objects are all between point one and point seven nanometers across."

"Nanites," Sam interrupted.

"Possibly. The objects do fit the size range but don't fit any known medical nanite specifications."

"Magnify," Sam said.

The holo screen displayed a single nanite with a complex structure composed of what appeared to be a metal alloy, some hard-to-see etchings, and tiny blinking lights.

"Are you able to zoom in closer, maybe identify the manufacturer of any of its components?" Sam asked.

"I'm sorry. I'm not programmed for that kind of task, but I'll be happy to help you with a diagnosis or medical protocols if needed."

"Is there anything else you can tell me about the nanite?" Sam asked.

The bot ran down a list of size, density, and temperature readings along with some molecular formulas to chemical signatures identified by existing medical banks.

"Can we do an extraction?" Sam asked.

"Working," the bot said, waiting a few seconds then repeating the same message. "This might take some time," the bot added.

Sam accessed the medical station log's specs for the beta nanites they injected Sam with earlier.

"You think it's the same nanites you were injected with?" Jeremy asked.

"I don't think so. Otherwise, the med bot would have it listed in the database."

"Working," the med bot interrupted, the same female face smiling on the holo screen above the kit.

"As far as I can tell, this boy is human, but based on the number of nanites, I think . . . Wait . . . Hand me the internal imager," Sam said.

Jeremy thumbed through the box and located a hollow metal rod with a small bead at the end and handed it over to Sam. The imager projected a transparent blue cone of light that Sam waived over the boy's head.

"What are you looking for?"

Before Sam could reply, the imager revealed tens of thousands of small flecks of light attached to the surface of the boy's imaged brain. "Holy crap!" Jeremy said.

"Yeah, I thought that might be the problem. Whatever these nanites are, I think they've taken over critical functions, neuropathways, sensory outputs, motor control. I just need an extraction."

"Ready," the med bot replied. A tiny mechanical arm rose from within the box, which the holo screen magnified.

The hand held a miniature tube with an even smaller magnet that rushed inside the blood toward one of the nanites. "Extraction successful."

Sam switched the display screen to compare the schematics with the nanites in the blood. After filtering through a list of specs, Sam said, "Whatever this souped-up version is, it's nothing like what I've got. Almost wish I did, but without the mind control. Whatever the med tech gave me is already wearing off."

"You think you can access its programming?"

"That's exactly what I'm trying to do. The fiber cable should be able to magnify the etchings, which are most likely the command pathways. And the light being emitted could be a host of things, but I think one of its functions is communications, a sort of Wi-Fi network it's using to interact with some external port somewhere. And my guess is that it's run on the same code I've been able to isolate from the array's systems."

Jeremy glanced at the lifeless boy, and its eyes opened. "You won't win," it said.

CHAPTER 22

Sᴇᴘᴛᴇᴍʙᴇʀ 3, 1984, ᴅᴀʏ 142, Fʀᴀɴᴋ'ꜱ ʙᴏᴅʏ
7:00 ᴀ.ᴍ.

THE ALARM SOUNDED. Quinn sprung up and eyed the room. He dialed Dr. Green and scribbled out the letters and array blueprints he'd tasked Dr. Green with delivering once Quinn hopped timelines.

They'd already looped another dozen days until they found Officer Channing's address, which was unlisted. The extra time they split between reviewing physics theories; pouring over vintage baseball cards, which were plentiful before eBay's business model decimated collector shops; and, of course, having a bit of fun along the way by pulling a few practical jokes. Quinn had found some of his lost humor, but he kept it within reason, not wanting to traumatize anyone.

They spent the next hour on the phone planning how to call the cops over like they did once before. But this time, Quinn would keep Officer Channing at his house while Dr. Green drove over to the cop's place.

Quinn peered through the peephole then let the officers

in, among them Mark Channing and the cop who looked like a stern Robert Patrick from *Terminator 2*.

The officers pushed their way through the door as Quinn stepped back. "So let me get this straight, Mr. Black."

Quinn already felt his blood pressure rising.

"You had just left a Broadway show, and for no apparent reason other than the fact that you were there, someone just shot in your direction?" Officer Channing said.

A phone call from Dr. Green interrupted them. He'd agreed ahead to call around that time just to confirm Officer Channing was at Quinn's place before he headed to his place.

Quinn turned his attention back to the officers. "I'm sorry, what were you saying?" His memory was already fuzzy from the several months' worth of days he'd looped.

Officer Channing repeated his last couple of sentences, and Quinn picked up from where he left off. After realizing he likely got a few key details wrong, he said, "I'm sorry, it's been a terrible twenty-four hours. You think you could come back tomorrow?"

The Robert Patrick–looking officer frowned, eyeing Officer Channing. "You called us. Remember?" Officer Channing's stiff partner said.

"I told you. It's just that—" Quinn hesitated, unsure which lie to feed them "—I'm still in shock from what happened. My mind's all over the place."

Quinn was right about that. His mind wasn't even in his own body. He forced himself down, feigning lightheadedness. "I'm not feeling well. Talking now just brought everything back into my mind, like I'm reliving it, over and over again."

They stood silent for a moment before Officer Channing sighed, closed his notepad, and stuck the pen back into the minispiral. "All right then, Mr. Black. We'll leave you to it. Someone will be contacting you from the station in the next couple of days," he said before pausing, "and I'm sorry for your loss."

Quinn wasn't sure if he believed him. He knew Officer Channing had been watching Dr. Green's colleague and was likely working with them in some capacity. Officer Channing already knew Quinn, but didn't bother to mention it. He was also a stone-cold prick in Quinn's original timeline. A wife-beating, child-abusing, scumbag of a man who didn't deserve to breathe the same air as most people who walked the planet.

But Quinn had also seen people change. He'd seen it in Officer Channing's son, Scott, and he'd seen others in various timelines transform from hideous creatures to the most gentle and caring humans on the planet. Maybe Mark Channing deserved the same deference as Scott. Maybe at this point in his life he wasn't too far gone. And in truth, Quinn wondered if anyone was ever too far gone.

A world away, in Brooklyn, Dr. Green finagled the lock on the shed door in Officer Channing's yard. He'd already inspected the house from the outside. Meredith was taking care of toddler Scott in the back room, so Dr. Green decided he had enough time to find what they needed.

After a glance in both directions, he jimmied the shed door, trying to open it with a makeshift lockpick. He dropped the pick then knelt to the ground searching for it and taking too long. Another minute later, he found it and went back to work opening the lock. A click sounded, and he opened the door.

Dr. Green kept the lights off and scanned the floor with

the flashlight but saw nothing but dusty gray wood panels. There were two tables, on either side of the room, and a few crates stacked in the center back. Underneath one of the tables, he found a large drawer with a gym bag.

Before he had a chance to get a good look, a noise boomed from the house. Dr. Green quietly closed the drawer and peeked out the window toward the direction of the sound. From the open curtains, Vladimir was saying something to Meredith, and young Scott's cries echoed from the back room. Dr. Green watched the scene unfold until Vladimir grabbed Meredith's arm. A tussle ensued.

Dr. Green debated on whether to assist. He needed to get the bag to Quinn, but only Quinn had the do-overs. For him, time wouldn't reset, and the Russian goon would go on to do whatever he had planned for her and the boy. He couldn't let that happen.

But then he considered what would happen if he did. Quinn might not get what he needed in this timeline, but either way, Quinn would leave at some point, most likely. If he didn't, then Quinn would be there to help build an array for this timeline's Earth.

He couldn't watch anymore. Dr. Green opened the bag before he left to see if it had what they had come for, then saw the gun. Dr. Green ran out of the shed and barged into the side door to the house, knocking it open. "Leave her alone!" he shouted.

Vladimir loosened his grip and turned toward Dr. Green, smiling. "Ah, yes. I figured I'd see you eventually. We're all tied together, aren't we, in life's intricate web. So you must have discovered the truth, then, about your colleague, no?"

"Let her go," he said, now gripping the gun with both hands.

"Now, now. A confused man like yourself shouldn't play with a big man's toys. You might hurt yourself. Just let me help you. Hand it over so you don't accidentally pull the trigger and blow your brains out. We wouldn't want that, now would we?"

Vladimir inched forward. "Come now. Hand it over. I won't hurt you. I promise. Let me get you some help. You're confused, no? Barging into the nice young lady's home. I wouldn't want you to get into any kind of trouble. I wouldn't want to have to call my friends down at the clinic, now would I?"

"Stay back. I'm warning you."

Vladimir advanced forward. "I'm trying to be nice here," he said with his thick Russian accent.

"I said stay back!" he said, cocking back the pistol hammer. "I'll shoot. I don't want to hurt you, but I will."

Meredith's mortified expression gave Dr. Green pause. He wasn't sure how much she knew about Vladimir, but she didn't seem too eager to watch him get shot either. Then Dr. Green heard the voice coming from the back of the room.

"Mommy, Mommy," the young boy cried. The boy gave Vladimir the distraction he needed. He lunged toward Dr. Green and grabbed the pistol but failed to secure it.

"Let go. I don't want anyone getting hurt," he said, now in a full-out brawl with Dr. Green.

Vladimir wrestled him to the floor. Dr. Green thrust his knee upward, clocking Vladimir in the chin. Vladimir moaned, spitting out blood. "I'm going to kill you, you little—" he said, showing his crimson-colored teeth.

A shot rang out. The boy squealed loudly from the back room. Meredith wailed, apparently thinking the boy might be hit.

Vladimir and Dr. Green both looked at each other. Dr. Green clasped his stomach then grimaced. Blood began to seep through his shirt and dribble over his tightly clenched hands.

"It's all right, Meredith. The buffoon just shot himself. Such a shame really. But don't worry. I'll clean this mess up," Vladimir said as Dr. Green closed his eyes for one last time.

CHAPTER 23

SEPTEMBER 3, 1984, DAY 142, FRANK'S BODY
3:03 P.M.

QUINN WAITED BY the phone all day, wishing he had a cell phone. He thought the worst, but had to check for himself to see if Dr. Green was still at Officer Channing's.

Before he left, he would mail the letters and blueprints he'd been writing during each loop to give the residents of the current timeline a fighting chance. He'd prefer to wait to see if Dr. Green was alive, but if he found himself locked up, or worse, it might be too late.

Ninety minutes later, Quinn sat in the back of the taxi half a block from Officer Channing's. He told the driver to pull over once he spotted Vladimir hoisting a large duffle bag over his shoulder and into his trunk. Once Vladimir drove off, Quinn ran to the front door, pounding until Meredith opened it.

"I'm sorry," Quinn said as a little boy ran up behind her and grabbed the bottom of her legs. Tears streamed down her face, mixing with the mascara and reminding him of dripping ash. Even in her current state, she was striking, all the more unrecognizable than his mother was at her age.

"What do you want?" she asked.

"Was Dr. Green here? Did something happen to him? I think that man that just drove off might have hurt him, done something to him."

He already knew the answer. Of course Vladimir had killed him, but he had to make sure.

"Please, just leave us alone. I don't know who you are. I just need to take care of my son right now."

"I'm sorry, I really am." Quinn considered his next question, almost asking her if he left a bag or if she had seen a bag, but thought it would be too much. "I just need to know if he was here. Can you at least tell me that much?" He went on to give a brief description.

She dropped her head. "Yes. He was here. But he's not anymore. Now please just leave."

Quinn walked back to the taxi that was still waiting for him.

"Where to?" the driver asked in his thick Pakistani accent.

September 3, 1984, day 143, Frank's body
8:03 a.m.

"We should do this together, double our chances," Quinn said, quickly scribbling the blueprints to the array to mail on their way out.

During the last few loops, he'd spent more time investigating the current state of affairs in 1984. He added a few more letters to his list of deserving benefactors once the timeline continued on without him. And he took pride in doing what nearly all time travel movies said he shouldn't.

They left thirty minutes earlier than Dr. Green had during the prior loop. Dr. Green couldn't tell him what had happened, but since it didn't work out the last time, leaving earlier made the most sense. If they failed this time, Quinn planned on leaving half an hour later in the next try.

An hour later, Dr. Green finagled the lock on the shed door in Officer Channing's yard. They'd already inspected the home from the outside. Meredith was taking care of toddler Scott in the back room, and they estimated they had enough time to find what they needed. Dr. Green charged Quinn with being lookout in case the situation changed.

After a glance in both directions, Dr. Green jimmied the shed door with a makeshift lockpick. He dropped the pick then knelt to the ground searching for it and taking too long. Another minute later, he found it and went back to work opening the lock. A click sounded, and he opened the door.

Dr. Green kept the lights off and scanned the floor with the flashlight yet saw nothing but dusty gray wood panels. There were two tables, one on either side of the room and a few crates stacked in the center back. Underneath one of the tables, he found a large drawer with a gym bag.

"I think I found something," Dr. Green said. Quinn moved from his watch post and glanced inside. Green lifted the gun, carefully placing it on the table facing away from them, then lifted out several stacks of police files directly underneath.

Quinn scanned through files while Dr. Green inspected a series of various-sized orbs. Quinn thumbed through one of the files, then another, until he'd seen the major contents of each. "This looks like dirt on half a dozen officers in Mark Channing's precinct. I think these files are being used as blackmail. And look at this one," Quinn said, flipping open the file to the picture of Officer Channing. "I think this one is blackmail on him. Maybe Vladimir is holding this over on him to gain his cooperation."

Dr. Green said nothing, still engrossed in inspecting the perfectly reflective spheres. "This is incredible. Look at these."

Quinn set aside the files and eyed the orbs, thinking about what kind of joke Jeremy might make if he were there with them.

"I remember the bomb in 2021 had something similar, but it was larger, spheres within a sphere. I think this might be too small for what we need," Quinn said.

"These may not be bombs, maybe more like collection devices of some kind. Maybe a siphon to gather dark matter. Remember the symbols from the book? Instructions for communication. Maybe these are communications devices or a combination of both. Do you remember how to activate them? I think we should just try to get a nice splattering of dark matter on you," Dr. Green said.

"You think that's safe?

Dr. Green chuckled, the first time he'd seen him smile in a while.

"You're the risk expert, but I don't think anything we've done since we've gotten back here is safe."

Something just occurred to Quinn. "Wait, what about radioactive decay? In the future," Quinn said, pausing, "you get exposed, we get exposed to polonium 210, which you thought was necessary to connect my mind to the holographic universe and tethered me to my original timelines."

Dr. Green thought for a moment, digesting everything they'd learned over the last two days based on their accelerated study of time travel.

"I think all that went out the window when you came

back in your father's body. I think it's dark matter, the exotic particles that must be stored in these orbs. How exactly they got there or how it works, that's a mystery for another day. But I think you're running out of juice, either that or universes in a converging multiverse. We're just going to have to get our hands dirty. Open these suckers up."

"Either way, we need to hurry. Whatever stopped you last time might happen again if we don't do something soon. You want to take these back and study them for a while or try to open them here?" Quinn asked.

A noise boomed from the house. Dr. Green quietly closed the drawer and peeked out the window toward the direction of the sound. From the open curtains, Vladimir was saying something to Meredith, and young Scott's cries echoed in from the back room.

"We don't have much time. Let's figure this out now. Vladimir's here."

Quinn thought back on how the orbs activated in the future, but they were multilayered. Only the external surface looked similar, but there were no protrusions on the smaller spheres in the bag. Quinn ran his hand alongside each one, rotating them, trying to twist them. "Maybe I can just rub them on myself," Quinn said.

"I don't think that's going to work. My guess is the spheres are made of exotic matter shielding, protecting the dark matter from escaping. You probably need to activate it somehow."

Quinn remembered something about Gary and Sam using water, nature's perfect molecule, to activate it. "Do you see any water around here?"

Dr. Green scanned the room but didn't see anything. Another boom sounded from the house. "Maybe there's a water hose outside," Quinn said, watching the window as

Vladimir began manhandling Meredith. "And maybe you can take this to stop him from doing whatever he's about to do," he added.

Quinn spotted the hose and opened the shed door, which immediately drew the attention of Vladimir, who looked straight at them through the open window panes. "Looks like you've lost your balls," Quinn said smiling, dashing toward the hose.

Dr. Green pointed the pistol in the direction of Vladimir. "Let her go if you want to live."

"You think I'm frightened of a special man like yourself? Just put down the little toy so you don't hurt yourself," he told Dr. Green.

Quinn's blood pressure shot up. "You really are asking for it, aren't you? Leave the man alone, and treat him with respect."

"Respect? Ha. Maybe you're both special. Let's see how you handle these." Vladimir lifted his arms, revealing two black Russian specials, MP-443 Grachs, one in each hand pointed directly at them. The guns resembled Glocks but were standard Russian issue. They were double-action short-recoil pistols designed to hold armor-piercing bullets with 18-round detachable box magazines. Quinn grew all too familiar with the specs during his past encounters with Russian goons.

"Get down," Quinn said. A barrage of fire opened up on them. A warm, piercing jolt struck Quinn's left shoulder, then his right. He stumbled. Something struck his upper chest, then in quick succession several more points of pressure threw him back. He stared up at the sky and breathed in the air one last time before closing his eyes.

September 3, 1984, day 144, Frank's body
7:43 a.m.

"We get in there, we get out. The water hose is on the outside of the shed. We don't dawdle," Quinn said to Dr. Green, quickly scribbling the blueprints to the array to mail on their way out.

A few minutes later, they hailed a taxi and headed toward Brooklyn. Once they arrived, they scurried into the shed, where Dr. Green picked the lock in seconds. Dr. Green kept the lights off and located one of the two tables and opened the large drawer.

Dr. Green retrieved the gym bag, lifted the gun, and placed it on the table facing away from them. Quinn dumped the stacks of police files onto the table for Dr. Green to scan them while Quinn raced outside with the orbs. He glanced toward the house, but all was quiet.

Quinn twisted on the water knob and let the hose inflate with water and placed the end directly into the gym bag. He exhaled, finally feeling a sense of relief, and stared at the orbs, hoping something would happen, a spark of light, a hum, a vibration.

He closely inspected the bag, watching the tiny woven threads of nylon dampen and leak like sieves, but the water level in the bag soon covered the smallest orbs and quickly rose higher. A few of the smaller orbs began to float, which shouldn't be possible, given their density. Soon after, a low-pitched hum activated and grew louder as each millisecond passed.

"I think it's working," Quinn said. Dr. Green came out from the shed to observe, and the noise drew the attention of Meredith, who was then on the porch looking upon them, holding the young Scott in her arms.

"What is that? What are you doing?" she asked.

"It's all right. We just came for this. We'll be gone soon," Quinn replied.

She stood immobile, watching as the hum grew louder. Thin horizontal sheets of blue light shot out from the center of several orbs. "I think it's working. I'm not sure what it's doing, but I think I activated it," Quinn said.

The blue light shot out further, this time solidly toward the horizon. The light shot back, restricting its range to a ten-foot diameter which engulfed only Quinn.

It was as if Quinn was in his own orb, and beyond it, time gradually slowed. Dr. Green was running toward him, and his stride eased to half pace. With each movement, Dr. Green took longer and longer to reach the next step until he stopped completely.

Another burst of blue light shot out from the remaining orbs. It rose, floating above the ground. Soon, the ten-foot bubble lifted into the air above the level of the house. Quinn crouched down to the bottom, his arms flailing as if he were worried he would fall from his current height above the Earth.

The motion halted, jarring Quinn, who steadied himself. Dr. Green gazed forward as Quinn stared down at him. Dr. Green spun around. He turned in the direction of Meredith, mouthing something which Quinn couldn't hear. Quinn strained to hear anything, the rustling of the trees, the wind, the birds. But it all fell silent. The orbs blocked all noise from outside the bubble.

Another flash of light shot from the orbs. They began floating within the bubble, humming in unison. A buzzing sensation penetrated Quinn's body followed by a metallic taste in his mouth and an indescribable smell.

Dr. Green's and Meredith's movement increased at the same rate it had slowed. Dr. Green's gait quickened to twice its normal rate as he stumbled around looking for the apparently invisible Quinn. It hastened further to ten times normal, then a hundred. In a few fractions of a second, Dr. Green left, and it was as if Quinn were watching a recording playing at high speed.

Everything in the immediate environment quickened. The motion sped to such a degree, Quinn could see only the changing position of the sun and then the rising and setting of the sun, moon, and stars. Time sped further. Days became weeks, then months. Soon the motion of the sun and moon transformed into a streak of light, and Quinn could no longer distinguish between day and night. They merged into a blend of one another, not quite dark or light, but a perpetual twilight.

The leaves vanished then appeared on the trees as they grew and morphed in shape with what Quinn assumed was trimming over the seasons. Colors shifted from green to brown then white. Seasons morphed into years all in less than thirty seconds.

Time continued its upward acceleration. Structures morphed. Houses reshaped. Nearby streets refurbished within Quinn's range. The hastening gathered momentum. Structures rose and fell, at first houses, then buildings, and eventually massive structures of reflective glass and metal.

A city sprawled and rose before him and around him in every direction. It engulfed him. But the motion hurried on, and eventually, the man-made towers fell. Those were soon replaced with giant statues that reached into the heavens, mountains of shape and structure, but those also fell, replaced by brown-and-red rock.

The sky's color shifted to more pink and reddish in hue. The solid line of the sun grew to half the sky. Then all Quinn could see was light, engulfed in the star he once called the sun. That light faded as well until all that remained were embers, and then nothing but blackness.

The bubble shook. Quinn trembled. A few more blasts of light shot from the orbs, and Quinn watched as the bubble vanished and his body atomized into nothingness.

SEPTEMBER 3, 1984, DAY 145, FRANK'S BODY
7:43 A.M.

Quinn filled Dr. Green in on what happened, how they found the orbs and what happened once he activated them.

"I was stuck there, unable to move outside the bubble. Time just moved faster. It sped up slowly at first; then everything sped up even more. At first, it was weeks, then years, then millennia. Before I knew it, the sun transformed into a red giant, and then I was at the death of the universe, the big rip. That's when the bubble popped, and I felt my body disintegrate," Quinn said.

Dr. Green listened quietly. His face said he was considering what Quinn said.

"The next thing I knew, I woke up in Dad's bed. We need to look at the book again, see what the symbols and the message was saying. Maybe there's a code or an activation sequence, or anything."

"It won't work if we just go back and try again," Quinn said to Dr. Green, quickly scribbling the blueprints to the array to mail on their way out.

"Are you sure? If you were caught in a time bubble, it sounds like you saw the death of our sun and then the universe. Your mind was thrown back into the timeline you're currently tethered to. But that might only be because you didn't have a chance to reflect on the day like you did before. Maybe you just need to relive the day and fall asleep."

Waiting one more day made the most sense to Quinn. If they were going to view the book, they'd either have to break into the library again or wait until the fourth and get there before Vladimir.

"You might be right. I'll try to wake up in the future tonight, but if I loop back, we'll need to review the book again, see if there's anything we missed." He cracked his knuckles and yawned, then thought for a moment. "Want to have some fun while we wait?" Quinn said.

Quinn deliberated more about how he could influence the timeline once he left. He'd only lived one day ahead, September 4, in this timeline, but collected all the upcoming events in the near future from all his prior research in the future.

Quinn increased his time travel benevolence, creating an even larger list. He knew most people would discard the letters, but worked out a system to have several sent over the course of a few weeks. And if Dr. Green survived him in each loop, he would contribute to the plan, which was to target specific high-impact events that could have the biggest positive impact for those who remained in the current timeline.

After an event-filled day, Quinn thought of the future in 2025 when he sat underneath the stars with Cameron and later talked to Jeremy, and then he closed his eyes.

CHAPTER 24

The Array, August 21, 2025, Day 1, Timeline 1
2:12 p.m.

"YOU WON'T WIN," the boy repeated, pushing his neck up from his position on the ground.

"Come on, man. Die already," Jeremy said. He aimed the last bullet in the chamber square at the boy's face and pulled the trigger.

Sam yanked the fiber-optic cables from the table then shoved the live wire they had used once before on the boy's face, down his mouth. Current surged through the boy. Tiny pops crackled around him, which Jeremy thought might be the sound of the nanites being fried. He could only hope.

For good measure, Sam shoved the boy into a nearby isolation chamber, part of the enhanced command room setting, and sealed it. They monitored the boy in the oxygen-deprived, force-resistant container until they were satisfied he was dead, for good this time. And if he wasn't, they could always flash heat the body then eject it into space through the exit tube.

Sam dove into code, examining the etchings from the

extracted nanite. Jeremy worked on restoring communications, which had been fully cut off after he partially restored them earlier.

Sam ran the extraction code, comparing the beta nanites with the one extracted from the boy. A holo screen appeared and zoomed in on the etchings. Sam's fingers danced on the keys and pounded out commands lightning quick. The holo fluttered multisequence lines that flowed down from the top in quick succession.

"I'm seeing a pattern between the etchings and the messenger's code," Sam said. "Look here." Sam pointed to a series of four-letter execution commands etched into the side of the nanite. "And the electron light sequence pattern that doubles both as a wave frequency emitter and a command trigger. And it goes both ways. This looks to be the reason it's been able to infect our system and why I've been unable to stop it up until this point. It keeps reactivating itself."

"You said you were able to quarantine the code," Jeremy replied.

A loud whirring sound emerged from the corner of the room holding the boy's body. "It's coming from the boy. I think it's trying to escape," Jeremy said.

Sam pulled up the array schematics within the limited confines of tier two. Despite being sealed off by the exotic matter walling, the room was still enclosed within the center of two adjacent segments, and Sam could access the systems, still operating all the equipment.

"Can't we just eject the boy?" Jeremy asked.

"We could, but we might need the nanites to hack the code."

"I thought we fried the nanites."

"Heated them more likely. Those are some resilient pieces

of hardware. But if I could trick the nanites into thinking one of my executables is from the messenger's code, we might be able to reprogram them and source back the code to find the rest of the message we saw earlier on the panel holo."

Jeremy wobbled, his knees buckling. A jolt of motion tossed Sam onto the floor. Sam got up, and then the floor shook twice as hard.

"It's gotta be the boy," Jeremy said.

Sam latched onto the station grip then fastened an emergency safety strap included with all stations. Several more trembles assaulted the room before Sam secured the position and logged back in. "I can't tell. But whatever's happening, it's impacting the entire area."

Jeremy leaned forward and pulled up navigation and communications. "I can't see anything on the sensors. You sure we shouldn't just eject the body?"

"No. Not yet."

"This thing might rip us apart if we don't," Jeremy replied.

"Just give me two minutes. I'm almost there," Sam said, tapping away at the commands. "You're right. I was able to quarantine the code. I put it in its own segmented folder, which should act as a partitioned drive. But I found something else. Or at least I think I found something else. There're two large programs embedded within our own systems code. And I think they've been there for a while."

"Didn't you say before that you managed to separate two distinct pieces of language within our systems?" Jeremy asked.

"Yes. But this is different. There are similarities with the one code that's been attacking the messenger's command and supporting our system. Based on my analysis, there's a sixty-three percent similarity between the helper code and the two programs, but there are major deviations."

Another bolt rocked the array. Jeremy tilted to the left, but the strap held him in his seat. He changed the screen display to show nearby space outside their location. Although they had no communications now between either Quinn's or Gary's array sections, radar tracking showed Gary close by, still orbiting the Earth-Moon system, with Quinn moving toward the sun.

"The antimatter injector coils are still blocked, but I've managed to open the release valves in case they activate," Jeremy said.

The release valves were a safety design built into the array in the event of excess storage. They could simultaneously convert a narrow beam of antimatter into high-energy gamma bursts and shoot them into open space, but they weren't intended to remain active for an extended period or deplete the entire storage capacity of the array.

A few alerts blinked on Sam's panel. "I think we have a problem," Sam said.

Jeremy executed a few commands of his own in a fruitless attempt to restore comms. He'd resorted to old-school emergency flash beacons to communicate with Earth but wasn't getting a response back. He knew they were likely scrambling on high alert as much as the crew of the array was.

"What is it now?"

"The nanites look like they've discovered what I was doing and are blocking my signal. They're sending execution commands to hidden pathways in several root systems."

"Can you stop them?"

"We'll find out soon enough," Sam said, pausing. "Wait,

the other code is sending out some kind of relay message, like it's blocking the nanite electron pulses."

Sam watched as two competing codes battled on the modified command line in front of them, twisting like a DNA helix constructed of symbols and commands. Whatever was happening gave Sam an opening to external systems.

"See if you can pull up the comms. I've regained some control," Sam said.

Jeremy clicked over to comms. The relays appeared active, but they weren't moving. It was like they were dummy pathways, a mock comms channel with no real function.

"This is bizarre. It should be working. There's no interference, but I'm not getting anything. Nothing. No radio, no frequencies of any kind."

"Is it turned on?" Sam asked.

"Of course it's turned on. What do you mean? Oh, hold on a second. No. It looks like you're right. We needed to reset the electrical pathways once the power was drained then restored. Checking comms again."

The whooshing sound returned. "Looks like the little bugger is going at it again. And something still is working with the comms, but I am showing green on power, so that's not it. You think it's time to flush the little man down the shoot?" Jeremy asked.

"Not yet. I still think I can find a work-around. If I can reconfigure a couple pathways, I might be able to—" A jolt shook the command station.

"I've just lost control of the antimatter injectors, and the systems aren't responding to my commands. I say we dump him."

"I can't. Not anymore. The messenger's code locked me out, and it's blocking the other code as well, and it's spreading throughout the system. But I still have control of navigation," Sam said.

"Then move us as far away as possible. I still can't pull up the other tiers, and we can't risk Earth getting hit."

Sam pulled up navigation on the holo screen and tapped in the command code to initiate full engines.

"I'll decouple the ports." Jeremy tapped on the control panel. "External clamps released."

"Engaging system drives now," Sam said.

A medium-pitched alert warning resonated throughout the room. A female computer voice said, "Engines engaging in three, two, one. Engines engaged."

Only three sections comprised tier two. With the limited mass, structural integrity and partial internal dampeners from the exotic matter allowed for quick acceleration, but it still gave a bit of a kick once the engines initialized. They were already strapped in, so Jeremy glared at the chamber holding the boy, watching for any change. Once the engines reached full capacity, the alert stopped and Sam went back to isolating the messenger's code.

"I've been able to block the signal, I think this time for good. Any luck on communications?"

"So far, still nothing," Jeremy replied.

"There's something else. I've also been able to isolate two separate video files encoded in the secondary code pathways. The execution files set the restrictions to lift if a specific sequence of commands was entered," Sam said.

"Can you play them?"

"Hold on. I just need to clean up a few pathways here. I almost got it," Sam said, pausing.

"There," Sam said as a 3D projected image appeared in front of them.

CHAPTER 25

September 3, 1984, day 146, Frank's body
7:43 a.m.

QUINN FILLED DR. Green in on what happened, from Vladimir, to the book, the orbs, and then the bubble in time. Quinn explained how he waited out the day and reflected on the future, but it still didn't work. Time threw his mind back to September 3 instead of the future.

He was uncertain on the specifics of how time travel even worked anymore. It was as if it kept changing. He didn't know why he didn't wake up one day forward, but figured it might have something to do with the orbs. But since he looped back to September 3, he needed to search the ancient book.

Quinn and Dr. Green quickly scribbled the letters about future events and blueprints of the array to give the current timeline a fighting chance. Then they assembled their crew of misfits and launched their impromptu miniparade as a distraction until capturing the manuscript.

After a successful heist, they returned to Dr. Green's office and got a second opinion from Dr. Green's Columbia associate, Hattie, on the time bubble. Quinn filled her in on all the key parts, this time keeping her focused on a few relevant pages, and questioned her about anything resembling time acceleration.

"You know a fair amount of Latin yourself. Where did you study?"

"Self-taught," Quinn replied.

She read over the passage a few times. Then her eyes lit up. "I think I found something here." She pointed to a page of glyphs and circles drawn within an ornate pattern. Each section of symbols contained different sizes of orbs. "I think it's saying that the functions of the orbs are tied to their size and cooperation, or something along those lines. They work together."

Quinn thought for a moment, wondering how this could help them. "I've been reviewing the passages on the last two pages, and they might suggest the messengers used the orbs or gained energy from the orbs." *Dark matter* was the more precise word in place of *energy*, which he omitted. "Do you see anything about how the messengers or followers might have used the orbs or gained energy from them in some way?"

She squinted her eyes, studying the symbols more closely, then flipped back to a section in the beginning. "This is interesting," she said, thumbing back and forth between the two sections of the book quietly for a full thirty seconds.

"This page here. It looks like instructions of some kind. When you look at it on its own, it reads like an introduction, but when you compare it to the glyphs next to each size orb, you can see the connection. And there's more."

Quinn's pulse rose. He pushed his chair closer to the book and smiled. "I think this could be it," he said.

They reviewed the symbols with the context of the prior loop's events and latest knowledge until they were satisfied they'd discovered the correct activation ritual. An hour before midnight, Quinn focused on the morning, remembering the day's events, and closed his eyes.

September 3, 1984, Day 147, Frank's body
7:43 a.m.

Quinn filled Dr. Green in on what had happened, from Vladimir, to the book, the orbs, the bubble in time, and the latest discovery from the ancient manuscript.

Once at Officer Channing's Brooklyn home, they broke into the shed, snatched the gym bag from the large drawer, and then raced outside with the orbs.

Quinn glanced toward the house, but all was quiet. He dumped the large orbs out onto the ground and placed the smallest two-inch spheres in the center. Water poured into the duffle bag, rising slowly until it covered their tops.

Once the orbs were submerged, a shockwave radiated from the cluster of small spheres. As a group, they floated to the surface, emitting the same blue light Quinn had seen in the prior loop. It reminded Quinn of fractal shapes in thin soap bubbles, dancing in myriad directions.

Quinn clasped the two center orbs and trembled as vibrations shook his body. The remaining orbs fell to the ground, with the two he touched hovering in place. The spheres separated horizontally then slammed together. A faint chime fanned outward from the clink, followed by a loud, piercing ring. Quinn covered his ears and closed his eyes until the noise subsided.

His eyes opened to a motionless world. He thought it

was like before and assumed he'd done something wrong. He expected the world around him would accelerate, but time held constant.

He plucked the two orbs from their immobile suspension in the air. The others in the bag sat on the skin of water-like surface pebbles stuck in solid concrete until he touched them. The water surrounding them floated like it was weightless and then froze again moments later.

The statuesque Dr. Green faced the orbs, unmoving. Meredith's visage and young Scott behind her stood perched behind the windowpane from their home, static as if captured by a photograph, transformed into a rigid effigy.

"Dr. Green!" Quinn said. The air muted his voice beyond a few feet with no reverberation or echo. He circled his friend, hesitating to touch him, but soon gave in. Quinn nudged Dr. Green, who quickly tilted. Quinn caught him before he fell and then lifted him back up into his original position.

Quinn returned to the yard and tapped on the two orbs suspended in the air which transmitted no sound, and then he realized neither did anything else. The world was quiet, lifeless, frozen. He wondered if it would remain encased in time forever and how far it extended.

He fiddled with the orbs for several minutes and then examined the areas around him, starting with the shed. Nothing worked. He flipped on the light switch in a fruitless effort. He grabbed the pistol and pulled the trigger. Nada. It might as well have been a toy.

The wind stood still, no movement in the clouds or sky, but he could breathe, so air could flow through his lungs.

"Hello!" he cried in what sounded like a whisper. No one responded.

He went indoors and inspected both Meredith and the

boy. He rummaged through the house to see what he could manipulate and what he couldn't. His original assumption held true. He could maneuver solid objects that were small, thin, detached, and flexible. Mechanical gadgets functioned if no power was required.

He assumed that time prevented all chemical and electrical reactions. Gravity worked on him, but the orbs froze momentum unless he was in direct contact with a small enough object or liquid. And time quickly recaptured anything far enough away from Quinn's grasp.

Quinn strolled the block and broke into the nearby homes and cars in search of life. For what must have been hours, he roamed the area hunting for movement. He couldn't be certain how long. Counting off the seconds was his only measure.

The sun held its position. The sky remained light, but there was no motion or sound except Quinn's voice. He observed what he could, grew bored, and then returned to the orbs.

He tried sleeping, but his mind raced. He stayed for who knows how long and kept his eyes shut until his nerves forbade it.

After a dreamless rest, he scoured the neighborhood for a bicycle then pedaled to Manhattan in the hopes of discovering more answers from the ancient manuscript.

The ride gave him a snapshot of the timeless landscape, eerily silent but beautiful. Urban decay stopped dead in its tracks. People froze midconversation. Cars rested on the roads with passengers in tow, quiet and stiff. And then there were distant landscapes, cityscapes, and bodies of water and puddles with small waves halted midcrest.

By the time he arrived near the library, hunger ravaged

him and signaled time's forward march isolated within his own body. He found a nearby convenience store and scarfed down the closest snack he could find, Oreos, which he washed down with some chocolate milk, which he could taste but not smell.

A short while later, he entered the library. A few people stood midstride. Others held books reading pages midflip. With no one to stop him, he pulled every manuscript from the section he thought was relevant and stacked them on the table near his seat. He scanned the same book they'd researched to death but soon turned his attention to the others he'd neglected.

He studied for hours, then days, weeks, and eventually years. He kept his range between Brooklyn and Manhattan and spent the bulk of his time studying, but soon ventured into more leisurely pursuits.

During the first few years, he tracked the passage of frozen time the best he could, estimating each eight-hour period. In the first year, loneliness strained his sanity, but he found solace in his usual routine, five days on, two days off. Then he added one full week off every month.

On his off weeks, he hunted down relatives and learned what he could about them. He cleaned up trash from the street and East River. He created elaborate explanations and stuffed letters about the future into thousands of mailboxes. He repositioned people and objects to avoid accidents when time resumed, if it resumed. He took up drawing and a few other hobbies. He tried painting, but the paint never dried.

During his weeks of work, Quinn hunted for the slightest clue for what to do once he came back. He assumed he had to die, and there were so many times he felt like killing himself, but two things stopped him. Isolation was his only impediment. He had enough time to research what he needed with no one getting in his way. The other reason was his ability to increase Earth's odds of survival in the current timeline if or when it resumed.

He knew he would die eventually. He was aging. In the early years, he shaved. But after a while, his beard had grown to Rip Van Winkle size, and there were a fair share of grays.

Years passed, and then decades. He accumulated knowledge and artwork. Quinn developed his creative skill and dove into refurbishing the city, square by square, home by home, and block by block. He assumed when time resumed, the amount of cleanup that occurred instantaneously would leave little doubt about the veracity of his time-travel letters.

The decades dragged on, and there were several days where Quinn had injured himself and wondered if he were close to the end. He'd broken bones, punctured his skin more times than he could count, and each time he thought he might die from infection. But he'd never been sick or developed a fever. His gut worked, but he wondered about the symbiotic microscopic organisms that lived inside his body.

He experimented with chemical reactions within his mouth, but that failed miserably. Eventually, he took time away from his studies, thinking a fresh perspective might give him better results. He started with every other month, then every other year. At one point, he took a decade off, but each time he returned, the symbols and glyphs told him the same thing.

Half a century later, he spent most of his time in meditation, only spending a few hours each day on study and city rehabilitation. Then one day, when he felt his life slipping away, he journeyed to the library for a final attempt and found the answer.

CHAPTER 26

Sᴇᴘᴛᴇᴍʙᴇʀ 3, 1984, ᴅᴀʏ 148, Fʀᴀɴᴋ's ʙᴏᴅʏ
7:43 ᴀ.ᴍ.

QUINN FILLED DR. Green in on what had happened, from Vladimir to the book, the orbs, the bubble in time, the frozen world, and his latest discovery from the ancient manuscript.

"We both have to touch orbs when I activate them. That's what we missed the first time. If we don't, whoever touches them will get stuck."

"Did you take anything good, maybe a Honus Wagner T206?" Dr. Green asked, referring to the most sought-after baseball card of all time.

Quinn hesitated, appreciating the company after a lifetime of solitude. Eventually, he smiled. "None of it mattered with no one to share it with."

They gathered their things and scribbled the letters to the world and array blueprints to mail before they left. A short time later, they broke into the shed, snatched the gym bag from the large drawer, and then raced outside with the orbs.

They opened the bag together, each moving half the

orbs into the same position like before. Once they organized the spheres correctly, Dr. Green turned on the hose. Water poured into the duffle bag, rising slowly until it completely covered the orbs.

Once the orbs were submerged, a shockwave radiated from the cluster of small spheres. The orbs floated to the surface and emitted the same blue light Quinn saw in the prior loop. Quinn and Dr. Green each gripped one orb then clasped them together.

The remaining orbs fell to the ground, with the two they touched hovering in place. The spheres separated horizontally then slammed together. A faint chime fanned outward from the clink, followed by a loud, piercing ring. They covered their ears and closed their eyes until the noise subsided.

They opened their eyes to a motionless world. Time held constant. Dr. Green plucked the two orbs from their immobile suspension in the air. A few droplets separated and floated as if in space, and then quickly froze again when his hand moved away.

"It didn't work," Quinn said.

"Give it a minute," Dr. Green said, rearranging the other orbs around on the ground. "Did you try activating the orbs last time?"

"Of course."

Dr. Green tried different configurations and activation patterns, but nothing worked. They tried for over an hour before they gave up.

Meredith and Scott stared at them frozen, perched behind the windowpane. The sun held its position. The sky remained light, but there was no motion or sound except their voice.

"We should go back to the library, see if we missed something."

Quinn sighed, changing the subject. "I want to try something. I'll run to the other side of the yard and see if you can hear me."

Dr. Green's face looked perplexed, and he watched on as Quinn strode backward until he was about fifty feet away. "Can you hear me?" Quinn asked.

"Why are you whispering? Speak up so I can hear you," Quinn assumed Dr. Green said based on the motion of his lips.

Quinn walked forward half the distance. "Can you hear me now?"

Dr. Green shook his head. "Can you hear me?" he replied.

"No," Quinn said, dropping his head.

They kept at it until they discovered ten feet was roughly the distance sound could travel between them. Quinn condensed what he'd learned the prior lifetime into a few hours. Dr. Green deliberated on the possibilities.

For the next day, they repeated prior experiments. They attempted chemical reactions in close proximity, manipulated objects, and arranged and tapped the orbs in various patterns. The rules held firm like before in Quinn's prior lifetime.

Once the novelty of discovering their limitations wore off, Dr. Green and Quinn completed a thorough search of Officer Channing's home. They didn't find anything, just the same stack of files they searched earlier in the bag, which still indicated Vladimir was blackmailing Officer Channing, forcing him to be a mole in the police department. Quinn suspected it was likely the reason Officer Channing didn't help them stop the 9/11 attacks in the prior timeline.

Whatever Officer Channing's involvement, it remained hidden. And there was also the possibility that those who knew about the orbs had changed Quinn's current timeline. Quinn hadn't seen anything to suggest that was the case, but without the internet, it was impossible to be certain.

At Dr. Green's prodding, they spent a few more days searching the shed and home. Eventually, they left.

"I think we should walk. It's very cathartic," Quinn said.

"There's no way in hell I'm walking from Brooklyn all the way to Manhattan."

"We have enough time."

Quinn could see anger welling in the usually practiced and even-keeled Dr. Green. But this was the first time he'd managed to bring someone with him. It wasn't a loop, but it was a lifetime.

"Not if I can help it. You know the old saying, 'Two heads are better than one.'"

Quinn relented and soon found bicycles for them both. Dr. Green tried to activate an old Harley on the off chance it might work, but had to settle for a mechanical ten-speed.

During the ride over, Dr. Green's expressions suggested he wasn't all that enamored with the silent landscapes or time-frozen oddities. He rode with purpose and often left Quinn behind, who dallied as he appreciated the sights. In his prior life, Quinn searched for overlooked scenes with each trip, but a few miles on the road with Dr. Green forced Quinn to pedal faster.

Saad's apartment was their first stop, but it held no clues. Then they headed to the police station. After locating Officer Channing's desk, they rummaged through his papers and found a few files that confirmed what they already suspected. But they found nothing that helped with their quest back to normal time.

"What do you think happens if I kill you?" Dr. Green asked.

"I'm sure I'll just wake up this morning like I did when I died last time. But I'm not sure that would help us if we don't find what we did wrong."

"What do you think would happen if you killed me?"

"Probably nothing is my guess, other than the fact I'd be stuck here by myself. I'd prefer to have some company while I'm here, so don't get any bright ideas. Trust me, you'll feel the same way in a few months."

"Don't you think things would just reset?" Dr. Green asked.

"Maybe for me, but I'm not sure about you. And I thought about killing myself last time, but I'm glad I didn't. It took awhile, but at least I was able to bring you in. We'll probably find something this time too," Quinn said, sensing the situation was taking a toll on Dr. Green.

They visited the library next. From there, Quinn repeated a similar strategy as before. They studied each book, but this time, they bounced ideas off each other. Quinn thought they made more progress, but eventually, they hit a wall like Quinn did last time.

The weeks dragged into months and years. Quinn rested more this time, trying four days on three days off and a three-week vacation every other month. At least with each other, they could play a few games, which the modified laws of physics made more interesting.

Years became decades, but Dr. Green's love of baseball cards never wavered. He'd secured a warehouse full of them and ventured further than Quinn ever did. But each time he stole something, he always replaced it with a letter containing valuable information if the owners acted on it once time resumed. And it was Dr. Green's habit that brought them to an antique bookstore in Upstate New York near where Quinn lived as a child.

The bookstore was unassuming. During the last several years, Dr. Green searched any bookstore in the Yellow Pages which even hinted at old books. But the Brown Leaf was all bestsellers and test guides. The only reason they were nearby was because of the vintage baseball card shop next door.

"I'm going to check it out," Quinn said.

He knew Dr. Green probably already crossed that one off his list, so he charged in without him. Quinn strolled through the aisles of books, thumbing through the occult section before a barely visible opening beckoned Quinn to visit.

Once he was inside, a small shelf with a peculiar shape caught his eye. "I think I see something over here," he called from the back, forgetting the distance limitation.

Dr. Green waited in front, but after a few minutes found Quinn. It was hard to see anything. The room was windowless and at an odd angle from the sun. A long, narrow hallway connected the far end of the room to a dark basement. Quinn felt his way into a narrow shaft that extended down a long flight of winding stairs.

Quinn ran his hands along the walls and came to what felt like an old bookshelf. It took a few moments for his eyes to adjust to the dim lighting. He soon saw the shapes of several large books with vellum and hide-skin bindings. He couldn't smell anything but imagined they might reek of must and mold if time flowed normally.

Quinn stacked the books by the door. Dr. Green tripped over them once he arrived. "Watch where you put those things. You don't want to end up in this place alone, do you?"

"Help me haul 'em out then," Quinn replied.

Once they brought all the books into the light, they realized they had something special. The set was opulent, more decorated than anything they'd seen in the Manhattan library. An oversized manuscript stood out. A watermark glyph branded two-thirds of its front exterior binding. On the inside page, they found a familiar set of instructions, a key, more detailed than the primary manuscript they'd been researching.

They spent the next few hours scouring the pages, reflecting on similarities. "I think I know what this means, but we need to get it back to the library and compare the two," Quinn said.

Quinn secured the book onto a basket and fastened it to the back of his bike. A few hours later, they plopped the book down in the main library's reference section and compared the pages. Quinn opened both of the center sections and pointed.

"See these symbols here; it's the space shuttle. I'm sure of it. And the date, September 5. I think it's saying that the orbs will send out a resonance frequency, but they require something else, a relay signal, to work properly."

"And you think that signal will come from the shuttle?"

"From the satellite that's being launched from the shuttle. The satellite will broadcast the frequency of a series of gamma ray bursts that will activate certain properties within the orb. Everything the orbs need to emit the dark matter is already inside. They just need the signal. And I think that won't happen until September 5," Quinn said.

Over the next few decades, they continued researching, but their reasoning didn't change. They lived out their remaining lives and found purpose in every day. Eventually, Dr. Green passed away. A few years later, Quinn followed suit.

CHAPTER 27

The Array, August 21, 2025, day 1, timeline 1
2:17 p.m. tier two

THE 3D IMAGE from the first message contained a male humanoid figure. The image blinked and shifted, not holding its intended shape. "If you're reading this message, exercise extreme caution. It's likely someone on your array has been sabotaging your systems."

"Now you tell us," Sam said.

The image cleaned itself up as it continued. "What you need to know is that I'm trying to help."

Jeremy noticed familiar features in the person speaking, but the image stood alone, like they were scanned separately from their surroundings.

The room jerked. Sam fell to the floor, and Jeremy rushed to Sam's aid. "You all right?"

The message continued while they spoke, briefly breaking up before it resumed. They both missed the last sentence.

"If you're seeing this message, it's because something triggered a malicious code. It won't stop until everyone on the array is dead. This was to be expected. I've activated a specially adapted program within your computer systems to help stop it. This message is on a low-bandwidth channel. You'll need to view another file to access my full-priority message. You can prompt the next message by using the proper command codes I've activated on the screen."

2:25 P.M. TIER THREE

From his modified port room, Gary attempted to read the system logs, but something locked him out.

Several sudden bolts rattled his section of the array. The loud buzzing of the cleanup crew nearby halted, followed by screams and a few cries for help. Seconds later, chunks of the array floated off into empty space near his window.

Gary's heart raced. He latched a few tools onto his belt and wheeled down the corridor. The scene was chaotic. Sections of wall crumbled onto the floor. Pieces of machinery cluttered the walkway. A few people up ahead scattered off in different directions, unsure of where to go.

Once he arrived, four people inside the damaged room held on to the crewmate. All of them wore breathing helmets and protective suits, but they could only hold onto their friend for so long.

Gary tossed them the sealant container, but they lost hold of it, and it flew out the window. He went for another one tied to his belt but lost his footing and went flying toward the hole.

In that moment, Gary regretted not getting to know them during the four years he spent on the array. He'd isolated himself inside his room and only interacted with the few crewmates who played the same games he did. The world owed its life to Quinn, and so did Gary. But at that moment, he thought he'd squandered it.

Gary was part of the greatest advancement in the world, but what did it all matter if he didn't share with others, engage more with people he cared about, seek out those who might bring each other joy. He'd lived his whole life in pursuit of the greatest game and wondered in that moment if he'd missed the greatest game of all.

"Hold on, I got you," someone shouted.

The array trembled. Their hold of Gary slipped. He went flying toward the hole and slammed into the other crewmate. Three of them collided and flew off into space. Gary spun and soon grew dizzy. He reached for the other sealant and sprayed wildly. His head rocked side to side, and he was unable to place his current position.

The cries faded, and the rocking stopped. He soon realized he'd been sucked out of the array and sealed himself out. But he was still attached and held firm to the sealant tube.

From his position, tier one was visible but moving quickly away in the distance. Tier two was closer but harder to see due to its size, but he could tell it was shaking wildly. Another knock jostled the array, sending vibrations through the thin filaments of the sealant that secured him to the array. His grip faltered. Another jolt shook him, and then everything went black.

2:32 P.M. TIER TWO

Sam called up the second message. A crisp three-dimensional image appeared with the same person from the first broadcast. The man stood tall, sure, and familiar.

The background landscape depicted a vast metropolis, inspiring tall glass and metal spires spaced between picturesque greenery and colorful flower gardens. In the foreground, several people roamed freely in various directions in the distance.

"My name is Ronan Black. For me, this is the year 2075. And if you're viewing this message, it means we were successful. But it also means there are others in your world and beyond who want to wreck your timeline and are willing to do whatever it takes."

The tube holding the boy rattled. Jeremy's pulse rose, ready to press Eject. The message fluttered briefly then continued.

A new figure emerged, smiling. "But it's not all bad news," the elderly man said in a calm, wavering voice.

Sam squinted. "Is that—"

"Quinn?" Jeremy replied.

"This is my son. If you don't recognize me, my name's Quinn Black. In my timeline, I designed the first array, but others soon followed. We've built a good life for ourselves in this timeline. And despite its problems, which are still quite a few, the world has gotten along pretty well. But it hasn't always been easy."

The floor trembled, but both Jeremy and Sam continued to look on.

"And we've learned that there are people from certain timelines who think their survival demands that they sow chaos in ours, in yours. We're just not certain why," the elderly Quinn said, pausing. "As far as we can tell, they are humans like us, or at least descendants of humans. We've tracked down their messages and their influence back through antiquity."

"Holy crap!" Sam said.

"But I know that they can only influence. They can't control. Their hope in chaos rests in others believing the lies they spread and giving into the division they sow. They are pernicious, and once they gain a foothold, they don't give up without a fight. And neither should you.

I've—"

The image collapsed. "You won't win," the boy laughed.

Jeremy hit the eject command, flushing the boy out of the array.

"No. Wait! I wasn't—" Sam said, interrupted by a fiery blast.

2:36 P.M. TIER THREE

Gary opened his eyes. A small boy floated by him. A blinding white light enveloped tier two and approached him. Before it did, tier one blinked and then vanished.

CHAPTER 28

September 3, 1984, day 149, Frank's body
7:43 a.m.

QUINN FILLED DR. Green in on what happened, from Vladimir, to the book, the orbs, the time bubbles, and his latest discovery from the ancient manuscript.

"That doesn't sound like me," Dr. Green said.

Quinn continued and went into more detail, giving him unique specifics about the baseball card collection Dr. Green acquired during frozen time.

"Maybe that does sound like me," he replied.

"The hardest part will be grabbing the orbs and disappearing until September 5. The glyphs suggested dusk would be the time to activate them. We just need to avoid something stopping us until then. That means we need to keep lookout, steal the orbs, then find a hideout somewhere, preferably outside of Manhattan. I'm thinking of Staten Island. No one wants to go there."

"You got that right," Dr. Green added.

"We find a crappy motel. Which won't be too hard. Check in and lay low. At 7:30, we activate the orbs, and I'll give myself a good dousing of dark matter, fall asleep, and then try to wake back up in the future, and hopefully my own body."

The rest of the day, they followed through with the plan. Quinn took in the year's loud outfits and retro signs, hopefully for one last time. They drove to Brooklyn, got In-N-Out, then found a dump in Travis-Chelsea, Staten Island. It had the smell of the water minus the view.

Just after 7:30 p.m., they opened the bag together. "Here goes nothing," Quinn said.

They each moved half the orbs into the right position. Once they organized the spheres correctly, Quinn turned on the tub. Water inched up until it completely covered the orbs. Once the orbs were submerged, a shockwave radiated from the cluster of small spheres. The orbs floated to the surface and emitted a familiar blue light. Quinn and Dr. Green each gripped one orb then clasped them together.

The remaining orbs fell to the ground, with the two they touched hovering in place. The spheres separated horizontally then slammed together. A loud chime fanned outward from the clink, followed by a loud, bellowing roar. They covered their ears and closed their eyes until the noise subsided.

The shower curtain rustled. A couple outside the motel began arguing, followed by a low plane that flew overhead from the direction of Newark.

"I think it worked," Quinn said.

They both dashed toward the window and cracked the curtains. The couple in the parking lot continued arguing. Sunlight faded fast behind the dull gray clouds hovering over the horizon.

"I'm turning in," Quinn said. He climbed onto the old mattress and tried not to think about who slept there before him or the bed bugs that might be hiding somewhere underneath. He thought of the night with Cameron, the night they spoke to Jeremy. He closed his eyes and fell asleep.

August 7, 2021, Day 2, Timeline 2
7:32 A.M.

Quinn stared ahead until Cameron's tight grip shook him from his stupor. The last thing he remembered was closing his eyes on the shabby mattress, but Quinn knew the exact time he'd arrived. The full brunt of the supernova was seconds away.

Quinn squinted, uncertain why he landed in 2021 instead of four years later, but he was in his own body after he built the array, so it was progress.

"Cameron," Quinn said, pausing. She kissed him before he could finish. He let the array do its thing before giving her the disturbing news.

A tide of light streamed in. The supernova's brightness exceeded the morning sun. The third time was best of all, but he still marveled at how the brightness rolled in like a calming white wave of ocean water. It sure beat Arthur Kill or Newark Bay.

Quinn let the morning play out a while longer, but his face couldn't lie, and he knew she could sense it. Quinn's brow furrowed. "There's something I need to tell you."

Cameron waited as he took longer to collect his thoughts.

"I've done this before."

She remained silent, just looking at him as if waiting for the punchline.

Quinn could tell she was still processing what he had said. He waited.

"What was the future like?" she asked.

"Better than the past. But that past does have its charm."

Quinn filled her on his trip to 1984, the manuscripts, the time bubbles, the next four years, and how the rules of time travel didn't make much sense anymore. He explained how he still wasn't sure what shot his mind back into 2021 or 1984. He told her the last thing he remembered was talking at night on the picnic blanket under the stars and then the phone call with Jeremy.

She digested what he said without saying much, and they both decided to keep it a secret until the following afternoon.

August 8, 2021, day 2, timeline 2
10:00 a.m.

Cameron sat in the pilot's seat of their chopper as they closed in on the city. Mammoth crowds gathered like a colony of ants. Gigantic balloons clogged the main arteries of Manhattan. As they flew in, the numbers of people exploded into a spectacle of epic proportions. More clusters of balloons became visible with inspiring and lighthearted designs.

Cameron led him toward the back entrance where they housed the parade float. "There he is," Jeremy shouted over the roaring crowd as Quinn made his way onto the float.

Quinn's face beamed, feeling as if someone had plucked him from his living room sofa and dropped him into the movie *Ferris Bueller's Day Off*. Two lifetimes of isolation made him enjoy the company more than any other point in all the years he'd lived.

Quinn climbed to the top of the float next to Jeremy and breathed in the night air. The sights and sounds made him forget his current dilemma. That moment was what life was all about, the reflection, the celebration, the gratitude.

Quinn decided not to tell the rest of his family about the problem until the following day. He attempted to return to the future that evening but failed. For the next week, he endeavored each night to return, but with no success. Eventually, he attempted to loop back.

CHAPTER 29

August 20, 2025, day 1, timeline 2
7:32 a.m.

DURING THE LAST four years, Quinn never managed to travel back to the future or discovered what threw him into his dad's body. He was, however, able to loop days, but only those after the supernova and within the present timeline.

With no impending threat, he took advantage of the loops, to enjoy both himself and his family. He researched the origin of the glyphs and those who still might be responsible for creating or working with them.

He spent his time relishing life and doing those things Jeremy always wanted him to do. He saved lives, but he also greatly accelerated the advancement of human civilization and technology.

Over the next four years in linear time, the array company expanded. Technological growth from Quinn's time looping exploded. In four short years, or long years from Quinn's perspective, mankind eliminated hunger, poverty, and most diseases. It found innovative ways to cooperate like it never had before. Incarceration rates plummeted.

Kindness, tolerance, and generosity proliferated. The dawn of a new era was just on the horizon.

In the recent weeks leading up to August 20, Quinn began seeing flashbacks. Bits of memories from August 21, ever so tiny, invaded his sleep and waking dreams. And when he woke on the 20th, they all flooded back in a torrent, every single one of them.

Quinn's eyes widened as he shot up. "We need to call Jeremy right now!"

"What is it?" Cameron asked, her eyes still partially closed.

"I remember it. I remember everything. We need to get to the array. I don't know how much things have changed since the last timeline, but someone or some*thing* might be trying to destroy it. We have to warn them."

They tossed on their clothes and hopped into the nearest transport tube. A few minutes later, Cameron and Quinn arrived at the space transportation hub in Long Island.

The station was tenfold the size it was in the prior timeline. A buzz of activity surrounded an immense garden that fronted the entrance, the most colorful public conservatory in the world. Lavender fields intertwined with rose bushes, and sculpted, purple shrubs formed a maze that led to the supernova theme park and alternating sections of greenery and shopping centers.

The scent of cotton candy and savory meats wafted along the artistic sidewalks leading to the launch center. Rows of painters and artists crafted masterpieces that rivaled those of Picasso, da Vinci, and others more recent. A slew of diverse families dallied nearby as they enjoyed the parade of nature, art, and eateries.

The closer they got to the entry doors, the more apparent

its immense size. The inside was also bigger than the first time and by an order of magnitude. Two high-speed rail stations met both sides of the hub. This time, they were in tubes, connected to underground networks that spanned the globe, as did all other space transportation hubs.

Inside, antimatter nodes rested on both sides of the entry point a thousand yards away. Each node spanned two hundred yards and was composed of twelve concentric blue chrome circles which housed powerful, targeted magnetic fields. Large floating tubes hovered above each node and funneled antimatter into the transport vehicles.

"Dr. Green! You need to alert the transportation authority and the Array Academy of possible sabotage. I need your fastest shuttle to get to the array," Quinn said.

Dr. Green turned toward Quinn and channeled his inner Doc Brown. He *was* the part, right down to the Einstein hair and shocked face with bulging eyes. Quinn half expected him to reply, "Great Scott!"

Dr. Green inhaled. His smile deflated into a look of concern. "In that case, you're going to need this," he said as his white strands of hair expanded like a porcupine getting ready for an attack. "I call it the Beast because it's the baddest beast of all the shuttles in the world," he said, walking them toward the direction of the vehicle.

Moments later, the vehicle inched up on the railing. The side hatch flipped up like an oversized DeLorean but with a sleeker oval shape in Tesla Roadster red.

"Go ahead, get in," Dr. Green said.

Cameron slid into the driver's seat as Quinn followed from the passenger's side and closed the door.

"Executing dual mode now," a voice said from inside.

"This baby will take you from zero to Mach 10 in a flash, so buckle up."

While Quinn entered a series of communications to Jeremy, Cameron entered the coordinates and synced their flight plan to the array. Seconds later, the Beast flew over the antimatter rings, inhaling a full engine's worth, then shot into space.

"Oooh. That's a smooth ride," Quinn said as the inertial dampeners fully engaged.

Once they arrived, a loading crew met them at the docking back.

"Captain," Sam said, speaking to Quinn.

"Please don't call me that. Leave that for the cadets."

"Commander, what's your status?" Quinn asked Jeremy.

The array's command room expanded with everything. And in the present timeline, the Array Academy had operated for nearly three years with a full military structure. Quinn ceded array command to Jeremy a year ago in preparation for launching the planet's fully crewed interstellar ship.

"We've located a foreign computer code within the array's systems. We've also found evidence of tampering on several decks on all tiers, but we've already reversed most of it. We did find evidence of several messages embedded within the array's systems," Jeremy said.

Sam continued where Jeremy left off. "The little you told us enabled us to quarantine the code. And you're right, there are two different languages. One is malicious, and the other, as far as we can tell, has helped block unauthorized attempts from the other one. Once we updated our system to recognize both, we located the compromised pathways and systems. It'll take a few days to sort through everything, but I feel confident the array is safe and able to fend off any new attacks by the code. And then there's this."

Sam activated the 3D holoprojector. A crisp three-dimensional image appeared with a young woman who stood tall, sure, and familiar.

The background landscape depicted a vast metropolis, inspiring tall glass and metal spires spaced between picturesque greenery and colorful flower gardens. In the foreground, several people roamed freely in various directions in the distance.

"My name is Laelynn Black. For me, this is the year 2075. And if you're viewing this message, it means we were successful. But it also means that there are others in your world and beyond who want to wreck your timeline and are willing to do whatever it takes."

A new figure emerged, smiling. "But it's not all bad news," the elderly man said in a calm, wavering voice. "This is my daughter. If you don't recognize me, my name's Quinn Black. In my timeline, I designed the first array, but others soon followed. We've built a good life for ourselves here, but recently, an organization known as the Way has threatened our way of life. We've learned that there are people from certain universes who think their survival requires that they sow chaos in ours, in yours," the elderly Quinn said, pausing.

"As far as we can tell, they are humans like us, or at least descendants of humans. We've tracked down their messages and their influence back through antiquity. They go by many names, the Way among them. We've come to the conclusion that they believe somehow halting the advancement of human civilization across the timelines will allow theirs to live on."

"Holy crap!" Cameron said.

The message continued. "Their desire for chaos rests in others believing the lies they spread and giving in to the division they sow. They are pernicious, and once they gain a foothold, they don't give up without a fight. And neither should you. I've included all the information we've gathered about them, including who may be working with them already and how you might stop them. Their recent attack on us won't succeed, but this is a battle that may be with us for some time to come."

The image collapsed. For the next few days, they eliminated all traces of the malicious code and put in safeguards to prevent another attack. They alerted authorities and developed plans for continued vigilance.

Later that week, Quinn pondered what might have happened in other timelines, in the worlds where he survived after being struck by the bolt of energy before he blacked out.

August 25, Timeline 1, Location Unknown
2:37 p.m. Tier One

Quinn's ears popped. His arms and legs refused to lift, like dense, old branches, still collapsed on the floor from whatever had struck him. He squirmed inward until his strength grew and he found the leverage to slowly push himself up.

The mini view screen displayed flashes from space beyond the fragmented array. One moment the array was there but growing more distant alongside Earth, and the next, the screen depicted all black.

A blinding multicolored light forced his eyes closed. A hum surrounded him, increasing in pitch and intensity with each passing moment. He attempted to tap the comms, but it was as if gravity was increasing, adding mass to his whole body, making him fight against a growing current pushing him in the opposite direction.

Streaming lines of light intersected his body and everything around him, changing in colors as the light surged past him. His torso jolted back, pushed by something, but what exactly, he didn't know.

Then just as quickly as the event began, it stopped. Quinn scanned the room. The holo display sparked, malfunctioning. He tapped the display controls triggering a cascade of sparks that singed his fingers. He activated the backup relays and external displays. They flickered on, but as they did, the floor buckled.

The hum returned, this time louder, deafening. Quinn covered his ears. The intensity exacted a cry which no one could hear. Blinding, hot light forced his burning eyes shut. His head bobbed from side to side as he gripped the seat railing at his hips.

The events repeated themselves, the rainbow-colored warm lights, the flashes, the hum. His head throbbed. For a brief second, it was as if he were detached from his own body then slammed back in. His eyes deceived him, showing him a series of events out of order, skipping around from one second to three seconds later then back again, like a twisted film spliced in random order but only for a few moments forward and back.

His own cries echoed around him, all at once and then none at all, alternating between eerie silence and a torrent of noise. And then finally it stopped, this time for good.

At first, there was darkness, a void of pitch without the slightest glimmer or inkling of something present, a hollow that exuded a sad, eternal loneliness. And then, as if a tiny seed born from something unearthed in a far-off land, an ever-so-slight glimmer emerged, faint at first, but warm and growing.

And then sound returned, as if the second creation birthed from the void, a distant echo, unsure and unsung. But like the light, it also grew, emerging from the vacant cries until it filled the room, and with it, life.

Quinn's head spun, but that soon passed. He steadied himself, opening his eyes and assessing the current state.

He finagled the control connections to the outside, rewiring the holo to view open space. A few stray sparks fluttered in random directions, but the holo flashed solid.

A familiar blue ball emerged in the center. But it was different, and it was not alone.

If you enjoyed this book, please share and show your support by leaving a review.

Don't forget to visit the link below for your FREE copy of *Salvation Ship*.

https://royhuff.net/salvationship/

Printed in Great Britain
by Amazon